EVERGREEN

A NOVEL

BUCK TURNER

For those who never lose faith.

THANK YOU FOR PURCHASING THIS BOOK

To receive the latest news and info, or to join Buck's team of beta readers, please go to:

www.buckturner.com

PROLOGUE

The Exodus

Memories are the monsters of the mind. They are pieces of our past, our most private possessions, lurking in the endless void between our ears.

My name is Cole Allen Mercer. My earliest memory is of my grandfather reading passages from the Bible as I drift off to sleep. He always began in the same place—John 3:16. After that, it was a bit of a crapshoot. Occasionally, he'd turn to Romans or the Book of Matthew, or Revelation if he was in a fire-and-brimstone mood, but he always ended with the same verse from Ecclesiastes. To this day, if I close my eyes, I can still hear his voice in my head:

To everything, there is a season,
A time for every purpose under heaven:
A time to be born,
And a time to die;
A time to plant,
And a time to pluck what is planted;

1

A time to kill,
And a time to heal;
A time to break down,
And a time to build up;
A time to weep,
And a time to laugh;
A time to mourn,
And a time to dance;
A time to cast away stones,
And a time to gather stones;
A time to embrace,
And a time to refrain from embracing;
A time to gain,
And a time to lose;
A time to keep,
And a time to throw away;
A time to tear,
And a time to sew;
A time to keep silent,
And a time to speak;
A time to love,
And a time to hate;
A time of war,
And a time of peace.

CHAPTER
ONE

GENESIS

It all began with a big bang!

The year was 1985. March 18, to be exact. I know because it was my best friend Max's birthday. He was turning sixteen and had been bragging for weeks about the jet-black '85 Porsche 944 his parents were buying him.

I had turned sixteen the week before, but instead of a Porsche, my parents surprised me by giving me the option of driving the station wagon on Thursdays. Lucky me. I hated that car; it looked like something an eighty-year-old woman with six cats would drive, so I respectfully declined and continued taking the bus instead. Most of the other kids that had already turned sixteen didn't have a car either, so at least I wasn't alone in my misery.

THAT AFTERNOON, I got home a little after four, changed clothes, and went into the kitchen for a snack. But before I could get my hands on the leftover pizza I'd hidden stealthily in the back of the fridge, the phone rang. Mom was sitting at the table and grabbed it before I could react. The next thing I remember was the sound of the phone hitting the floor, followed by a scream so terrible to this day the reverberations still echo in my head. It was the beginning of a nightmare from which I still haven't awoken.

My father, Captain Stephen P. Mercer, was thirty-nine years old when the 737 he was flying went down in a forest outside Albany, New York. FRIGHT 119 was the headline on the front page of *USA Today*. It was the worst air disaster since the American Airlines crash that killed two hundred seventy-two outside Chicago in 1979.

After several months of investigation, the NTSB finally determined the cause of the crash was a faulty thrust reverser on the jet's right-side engine, which had deployed unexpectedly shortly after takeoff. All one hundred eighty-three passengers and ten crew members died on impact.

My father was an excellent pilot with an exemplary record. Trained in the United States Navy, he had flown F-14s and F-15s worldwide and had five thousand flight hours under his belt. He knew every trick in the book, inside and out, which is why the accident was so difficult to comprehend.

I thought the NTSB spokesperson said it best. "Captain Mercer, as experienced a pilot as there was, died in the crash of Flight 119 fighting the one enemy he could not defeat— aerodynamics." I hate to admit it, but even the greatest among us are slaves to physics, and none of us are immortal. As I would later understand, no one could have overcome the deployment of the reverser. Essentially, it was the kiss of death.

The jet manufacturer scrambled to reengineer the design of the reverser after the accident and set up a foundation in my father's name, which was generous of them, but it made me reconsider the value of life. It's impossible to know how many lives it saved in the years following the accident, but I'd say hundreds, if not thousands, perhaps more. It's ironic when you think about it. Some people must die so others can live. That's quite the paradox. Perhaps I should have been happy for the lives that were saved, and I was. But it couldn't bring my father back, and that's really all I cared about. I guess in the end, we're all selfish in our own way, aren't we?

It took my mother three days to come to grips with the fact that she would never again see him walk through the front door and another month before the crying relented. I remember sitting in my room at night, holding the pillow over my ears, praying for silence. God, what I wouldn't have done to stop her crying.

We buried my father with full military honors on a rainy Tuesday morning in a quiet corner of Rochester's Riverside Cemetery. Hundreds of people turned out to pay their respects.

I suppose if anyone asked, his death had the most significant impact on me, though I internalized most of it. My mother was inconsolable, as any wife would be when her husband of twenty years dies. My sister was only four, so she didn't fully grasp the gravity of the situation. But at sixteen, I was clearheaded through the entire ordeal. I didn't cry much, not even when they lowered his casket into the ground. I hadn't when Grandpa died in '82 or my grandmother two years later.

I didn't shed a tear. According to my dad, crying was a sign of weakness.

The closest I came to breaking down came several weeks later. I had figured we would stay in Rochester forever, or at least until I finished high school, but I kept forgetting it wasn't my mother's home. She had grown up in the South, in a small out-of-the-way place called Evergreen. According to her, we had visited a couple of times when I was young, but that was when my grandparents were still alive. After they passed, Mom didn't see any reason to go back—something about it being too painful. But then, out of the blue, she told me we were leaving Rochester, and moving to Evergreen.

Talk about a punch to the gut.

CHAPTER
TWO

SATURDAY, AUGUST 03, 1985

Some events are so significant that you are forced to refer to every moment in your life as *before* or *after*.

"Will you hate me forever?" My mother's tone was bleak. I knew she wanted me to meet her halfway, but I was stubborn.

I stood at the window in my room, the one with the crack in the pane, and stared out into the street where my friends were playing football. I'd never been the jealous type, but at that moment, I envied them. None of them had lost their dad, and none of them had the dread of moving away from the only home they'd ever known. They'd all go to high school and graduate and someday look back on their time in Rochester and remember the days of their childhood fondly. I, on the other hand, would never have that luxury.

Without looking at her, I shrugged with indifference. The last thing I wanted was to give the impression everything was okay between us.

She sighed. "All right. I'll leave you alone, but we're leaving in fifteen minutes, so say your goodbyes."

I could hear her tapping the face of her watch with her fingernail. God, it was like nails on a chalkboard. My skin crawled. I should have been angry, but I wasn't. That shipped had sailed, and in its place was a void of indifference. Besides, I still held to a glimmer of hope she would change her mind— an optimist to the bitter end.

When I was sure she had gone, I said goodbye to my room for the last time, switched off the light, then grabbed my bag and made for the door.

I felt marginally better once I was in the car, comfortably wedged between my goose-down pillow and the red-and-white Coleman cooler. But as I looked around, I noticed something was off. "Wait!" I cried. I jumped from the car and crossed the yard. And there, in the backyard, was Roger, Tabitha's favorite stuffed animal. She had been playing with it earlier in the day while Mom and I loaded boxes into the moving truck.

"Here," I said, handing it to her as I returned to the car.

Tabitha smiled, hugging the animal as if it was her only friend in the world.

I was certain Mom was looking at me in the mirror, but I managed to avoid eye contact.

It was five after six when we backed out of the drive, and despite my desire to stay, I could do nothing but watch helplessly from the back seat as the only home I had ever known slid away in the rearview mirror. To add insult to injury, a twelve-hour journey still lay ahead of us. I shuddered at the thought.

The first leg of our exodus took us south on I-390 to

Harrisburg, Pennsylvania. From there, we traveled southwest on I-81, stopping somewhere in the West Virginia mountains to stay the night. Early the next morning, we were at it again, driving until we reached Kingsport, Tennessee, then proceeded south again on I-26 until we reached the exit.

Evergreen was only a few miles from the interstate but far enough to dissuade tourists from stopping to fill up on gasoline or to stretch their legs. There was only one service station, and you had to go all the way into town to find it, and there were no fast-food restaurants or hotels either.

The one thing it had was a church—a large wooden building painted chalk white with a steeple, atop which stood a cross made of bronze that blazed in the sunlight. And above the double doors, proudly displayed in stark black letters, was the name—WHITE HALL BAPTIST CHURCH. It was the first thing that greeted you when you passed the sign announcing your arrival. You couldn't miss it if you tried.

Beyond the church, the road descended through a cut in the trees, turned right, then slipped narrowly beneath a train trestle. Beyond it, in a depression in the earth, lay the town of Evergreen, rising in layers against the backdrop of the Blue Ridge Mountains.

It was almost noon when our car found Corwyn Street. The sun shone brightly overhead, which I hoped was a good omen, and if not, at least I felt less depressed when it was out. It had been hazy all summer, but thanks to the cold front that had pushed through overnight, the air was clear and crisp, and the sky had returned to its usual indigo hue. Shrinking puddles, the last shred of evidence of the overnight rains, littered the ground.

Mom and Tabitha had been chatting since we left the

interstate about a Barbie doll they saw in the store a few days earlier. I tried my best to tune them out. From my cramped position in the back seat, I was feeling more animal than human, and knew that if I didn't get out soon and have a few minutes to myself, I was going to lose what remained of my already-troubled mind.

Out of nowhere, a pair of teenage girls appeared on the side of the road.

They were my age, with blond hair and tanned skin. One of them had freckles. My brain buzzed to life. They were sitting on a green park bench outside a diner on the corner of Corwyn and Lewellyn. They smiled and waved. I did the same. I could only hope Mom hadn't noticed. In her eyes, I was still a baby. She had said so the week before. But I was a couple of years removed from puberty and counting, and the way I saw it, I was but a stone's throw from manhood.

"Mommy, I have to use the bathroom." Tabitha clutched her navy corduroy pants as the station wagon lurched forward under the traffic light.

I rolled my eyes.

The girls disappeared behind us along with my smile.

"Okay, sweetie. I think we're almost there," Mom replied cheerfully as she hung a right on Old Lockwood Road. I studied her face in the mirror. She appeared as relieved as I was. Not because of the destination, per se, but perhaps because the journey was over.

Traditional two-story homes with lush green lawns flanked the long street that snaked up to a part of town known as the Bluff. Most of the houses were older, looking as though they had been there for a century or longer. Many were painted white, but there was a smattering of yellow, green, pink, and lilac. It was like looking into an Easter basket. Black shutters and steep gabled roofs dominated the structures. Brick chimneys stood at one end, or both, which I imagined came in handy in the winter. But the ones I admired the most were held captive by masses of thick ivy that climbed up the sides and over the walls like creeping death.

"Well, there it is," my mother boasted, looking through a bug-splattered windshield at a nineteenth-century Victorian.

I leaned forward. At a minimum, it needed a fresh coat of paint. The swing on the front porch was broken and would need to be repaired, but overall, it was not as bad as I had imagined.

"Don't you love it?" Mom said, taking a closer look. It was apparent she was trying to be positive, perhaps for Tabitha's sake, but I sensed the uncertainty lurking beneath the surface.

"I like the tree." I was looking at the black maple in the front yard, which by my estimation was at least thirty feet tall. Finding something positive to say was critical, or she would be on my case for the rest of the day.

Tabitha clapped her hands playfully. "Doll house." She beamed. Evidently, she had forgotten about her need to find a bathroom.

"Good girl, Tabby cat," Mom replied in a high-pitched voice, the kind you only use when speaking to children. Sometimes I thought she did it just to annoy me. She sighed. "I wish your father were here to see it." She glanced at me in the mirror. Her timing couldn't have been worse.

"Yeah, but if Dad were still alive, we'd be at home where we belong, wouldn't we?" I forced myself out of the car and slammed the door with unnecessary force.

The moving truck ahead of us in the driveway had been

there for at least an hour. The gate was down, and half of our stuff was already inside. Tabitha's bed was sitting on the tailgate along with a nightstand and dresser that were to be unloaded next.

I drew in a breath of mountain air, hoping to calm my nerves, but it reeked of pine and rotting flesh. It was trash day, and the cans were still out at the ends of the driveways. Across the street, one lay on its side, its contents strewn along the sidewalk and picked through in the predawn hours by dogs or raccoons or whatever other godforsaken creatures roamed the woods in these parts.

I followed the movers into the house. The first thing I noticed was the unmistakable odor of mothballs, which I presumed was a holdover from the old lady that lived in the house before us. Her name was something forgettable, like Jones or Smith. I'm terrible with names, especially last names, but Mom mentioned her in one of her long-winded conversations with Susie, our realtor.

Tiny particles of dust floated effortlessly in streams of yolk-colored light that bled in through the tobacco drapes. I buried my nose in the bend of my arm and made for the staircase. I raced immediately to the second floor with a single purpose in mind. There was a room at the end of the hall painted olive green. It had a wooden ceiling fan in the shape of an old airplane propeller, which I found interesting, and there was a large picture window that overlooked the backyard.

"This one's mine," I declared, loud enough so the entire house could hear me. To make sure, I stomped my foot on the hardwood floor, staking claim to it before anyone else had the chance.

I stood by the window and peered down at our yard, which was framed by a wooden fence on two sides, and at the back by a creek that meandered along the edge of the property. Beyond it lay a sea of white pines, firs, beech, and birch trees that stretched out in undulating waves as far as the eye could see. Near the top of a nearby ridge, hidden almost entirely by a canopy of emerald-green foliage, stood a small cabin. If not for the thin ribbon of smoke coming from its chimney, I might not have noticed it at all.

"Good choice," came the voice of my mother as she appeared there in the doorway behind me, Tabitha clinging to her leg like a primate. "I'll take the one at the other end so I can be closer to Tabby."

"Good idea," I said automatically. That was the first thing she had said all day I agreed with.

WHEN WE FINISHED UNLOADING and the moving truck left, I started digging through the boxes to find my comics. I had been a fan of Marvel comics since I was a kid, and although I was sixteen, I still enjoyed reading them.

"There you are," I whispered as I found the box labeled COLE'S STUFF. I ripped off the piece of duct tape, then sat down in the chair and dug through several layers of Nintendo games and *Sports Illustrated* magazines until I found what I was looking for. It was the first moment of peace I'd had in a week.

I had opened the cover to my favorite episode—*Iron Man* #128, "Demon in a Bottle"—when the doorbell rang. I could hear the click-clack of my mother's heels on the hardwood as she crossed the foyer. Straining to listen, I leaned an ear toward the door and held my breath.

"COLE!" My mom's voice pierced the silence like a knife. Usually, a shout like that meant I was in trouble, but this was more of a *get your ass down here and introduce yourself to our guests* kind of tone.

I groaned, tossing the comic on the bed. "What now?"

I descended the stairs with heavy footsteps to let her know I wasn't happy about the interruption and made for the door. I slipped in my socked feet at the landing and had to catch myself on the railing to keep from falling, then resumed my approach. But even before I got to the door, I saw a woman in the open space, holding a casserole dish. she wasn't alone. Someone was standing behind her, I now noticed, which piqued my interest. I knew how my mom felt about my long hair, so I quickly swept it away from my eyes. The last thing I wanted was to be scolded in front of strangers.

"This is Cole, my oldest," she said proudly as I slid into the space beside her. I was taller than her now and had been for a couple of years.

"Hello, young man. I'm Cindy Davenport, and this is my daughter, Amanda."

Amanda poked her head out from behind her mother and waved.

The sight of her nearly stopped my heart. I managed to raise my hand and conjure what I presumed was something resembling a wave, though I couldn't be sure.

Cindy Davenport was a fortysomething woman with a bit of a weight problem, likely the result of years of excessively gorging herself on cholesterol-laden casseroles like the one she now held in her chubby hands. It should have been the first thing I noticed, but her perm, which she wore like a badge of honor, was the real star of the show. I wanted to turn away, but it was mesmerizing, like that one house in the neighborhood that always goes overboard on Christmas lights. There was simply no escaping it. At least it took the attention from her lazy eye, which now and then slid away from its intended target like the broken arm on a record player. She reminded me of the mutants from my comic books, the kind with two heads, an unintended result of a government experiment gone wrong. She spoke with a voice thick as molasses and had perfected the art of adding syllables to words where none were required. I could tell by the gleam in her one normal eye she relished the opportunity to gossip and had only shown up on our doorstep with one goal in mind —to have my mother regale her with the gory details of my father's death.

Her daughter, on the other hand, was as perfect a creature as God had ever made. She was nothing like her mother, and it made me wonder, albeit briefly, if she had been adopted. But quickly my curiosity was quelled as I realized they shared a nose. A perfectly lovely nose. Thank God it wasn't the eyes.

Moreover, she was nothing like the vampires in Rochester, with dark hair, pale skin, and hatred for the sun. She was tall and lean, athletic even, and had sparkling blue eyes. Her blond hair shimmered in the sunlight like strands of pure gold, the ends dancing playfully on the soft curves of her tanned shoulders. It was rude to stare, but I appeared to have lost all control of my mind.

"I'm afraid he's not much of a talker." Mom looked at me with pity as she reached up and unsuccessfully swatted at the wispy strands of brown hair that were now back in front of my eyes. Was I the only one who realized I was sixteen?

Luckily, the sound of her voice broke the spell. "Pleasure to meet you." I flashed a look of reproach in my mom's direction. "I'd love to stay and chat, but I'm afraid I'm a little preoccupied with the unpacking." I could tell my words had successfully torpedoed my mother's claim of me being shy. Mission accomplished.

"I could help," offered Amanda, springing to life. Her eyes beckoned. "That is, if you don't mind, Mrs. Mercer?" She laced her hands innocently while she waited for the all-clear.

I must have had quite the look of shock on my face. I wasn't accustomed to girls wanting to do anything with me, let alone come to my room, but my recent emergence from that awkward postpubescent stage dominated by acne and oily skin gave me hope.

I stared expectantly at my mom while she pondered Amanda's request.

"Not at all dear, and how polite of you to ask." She glanced at me and tilted her head ever so slightly toward the stairs. "And where are my manners?" She turned back to Cindy. "Please come in. I'm so glad you stopped by. Let's get that casserole in the oven before it gets cold, shall we?"

If there's one thing I hate, it's a casserole. After my dad died, I remember the kitchen being full of ceramic dishes and glass nine-by-thirteens, the contents indeterminable but looking as though they contained everything but the kitchen sink. I wish people had a better way of offering their condolences. A phone call or a well-written letter would have sufficed, but no, it had to be food. Ugh.

Amanda wasted little time in separating herself from her

mother. She slid past me and bounded up the stairs as her mother disappeared into the living room, still holding the casserole dish like an offering.

"I like your room," she chirped as she scanned the space. She went straight to the window. "My house is just there." She pointed to a lemon-yellow two-story just up the street. It was almost the same color as her mother's hair. I stifled a laugh.

I hadn't noticed when she was on the porch, but now that I was close enough to smell her lavender perfume, I realized we were nearly the same height. It would have been awkward, at least for me, if she had been any taller or me any shorter. I straightened my back, which gave me at least another inch. I was five ten, slightly above average for most grown men, but I was waiting for that second growth spurt to push me over six feet, which I assumed was still at least another year away. My dad had been six two, so I had at least a fighting chance.

"You're into comics?" She spotted the one I left on the bed.

Damn. My brown eyes must have been as large as saucers. If I'd known a girl was going to be in my room that day, especially one as gorgeous as Amanda Davenport, I would have burned the damn things or at least hid them at the bottom of the closet. I tried to play it cool. "Um, no, not anymore. They're..." My voice faded as I searched for a plausible explanation.

"Punisher, awesome!" She sat down in the chair and rifled through the open box.

"You like comics?" None of the girls in Rochester had been into comics, even went out of their way to tease me about it. It was part of the reason I had anger issues.

"Who doesn't?" She eagerly thumbed through the pages.

I pinched myself to make sure I wasn't dreaming. Now for the most important question of all.

"Okay. So if you like comics so much, are you team Marvel or team DC?" I was casual about it, but I had to ask. It mattered.

She looked up. "Is that even a question? Marvel of course," she replied without hesitation, and her eyes fell. "No offense, but DC loses me with the capes."

Oh my God. I'm in love.

"So what's it like in New York City?" She quickly changed the subject as she continued to flip through the pages. Maybe she was trying to play it cool, but I could tell by the tenor of her voice this was what she really wanted to talk about.

"Hell if I know," I replied indifferently, grabbing a T-shirt from one of the open boxes. "I grew up in Rochester."

"Where's that?"

"Other side of the state."

"Oh." I detected a hint of disappointment. "But you've been to the Big Apple, right?"

She found me fascinating because of where I was from and the places I had been, though to be honest, I hadn't been to all that many places. Still, I had underestimated the advantage that came with being from a place like New York. It held a certain mystique, and whether or not I lived in the city didn't matter.

I wondered why everyone who hadn't been to New York City insisted on calling it the Big Apple. I hated everything about the city—the people, the buildings, the insane time to get from place to place—there was nothing about it that did anything for me except leave me frustrated to the point I wanted to crack my head against the subway wall.

"I've been there a few times," I said, deciding to keep the conversation going.

"What was it like?" By the glint in her eyes, I could tell she imagined it the way most people do—a magical place with glittering skyscrapers, Broadway shows, and high fashion. What a load of crap. It was nothing more than an over-crowded, crime-infested concrete jungle where the sun never reached the streets—a sprawling, twisted prison of flesh and steel—ready to devour anyone foolish enough to set foot inside the city limits.

"Busy," I replied, choosing my words carefully. I didn't have the heart to tell her the truth. "So what do you do around here for fun?" I thought it best to steer the conversation in a safer direction.

"Not much." She frowned. "There's a theater in town and a diner. They have good burgers and milkshakes if you like that sort of thing. Oh, and they're building a skating rink," she added with a smile. "But it won't be open until spring."

"Ice-skating?" Suddenly this town wasn't a complete disaster.

"Roller-skating." She dashed my hopes. "It doesn't get cold enough here for ice-skating, at least not normally, but they do have an ice rink open in the square during the holidays."

I had been a hockey player since I was old enough to stand. I wondered now if anyone in Evergreen even knew how to spell the word *hockey*.

"So do you need any help?" Her tone was bright again.

"Do you *want* to help? I mean, if you'd rather go down-stairs, we could..."

"No! I mean, I don't want to go downstairs," she

19

confessed. "Not that I don't love my mother, but if I have to lie one more time about how much fun I had at church camp this summer, I'm going to go mad."

"Oh God..."

"Exactly. Not that I don't believe in God or anything, it's just... do you believe... in God?" She lifted her gaze to me.

I couldn't believe she had come out and asked me like that. How direct. Where I was from, most people kept that kind of thing to themselves.

"Does it matter?"

"No. I was only curious," she said, then glanced away. "Everyone here does. They think you're the devil if you don't." She cracked a smile, then returned to the comic.

I turned and gazed out the window. A pair of blue jays flew across the yard and landed on a rock near the creek. Birds had always fascinated me. "I used to think there was a God when I was a kid," I said after a long pause. "My dad was a pilot. You probably already know he died."

"Yeah, I heard. I'm sorry, by the way."

"Thanks. When I was younger, my dad flew a lot. At night, I remember hearing my mom asking God to keep him safe. After a while, I believed Mom and God had worked out an agreement. Stupid, isn't it?"

"I don't think so," she said thoughtfully. "We believe all sorts of things when we're little. I mean, I used to believe in Santa and the Easter Bunny."

"The day of the crash, I remember asking myself whether I had heard her pray the night before, as if one more prayer would have made a difference." I chuckled. "Either way, like I said—stupid." I turned from the window. "You still want to help?"

"Um, sure."

"All right. Start anywhere you like."

"Got a pocketknife?" she asked as she rose to her feet.

That confirmed it. In all my sixteen years, I had never met another girl like Amanda Davenport. She was the trinity of perfection—gorgeous, liked comics, and knew how to use a pocketknife. If we had been eighteen, I would have dropped to one knee and asked her to marry me right then and there.

I tossed her the pocketknife my dad had given me when I was ten. It was a four-inch Buck knife with a wooden handle. It was a little beat up, but I kept the blade sharp.

"Do you know who you have for homeroom this year?" She cut the tape across the box labeled TROPHIES AND AWARDS. "I think I have Mr. Simon. He was my geometry teacher last year."

"Um..." My class schedule had arrived by mail the week before, and I had managed to sneak it into my room before my mom got hold of it. I rummaged through a nearby box until I located it, then scanned the paper and found the name Del Richardson.

"Del the Smell." She chuckled. "Too bad. But my best friend Kimberly has him. You'll like her. What about the rest of your classes?"

Rather than read them off one by one, I handed her the piece of paper so she could examine it on her own.

"Well, we have gym together with Phelps—fifth period," she said happily.

That was perfect. I was an athlete, and she at least had the frame for it. I was glad it wasn't English. When it came to distinguishing a participle from a prepositional phrase, I was hopelessly lost.

"We'll see each other a lot, I'm sure. Evergreen High isn't that big. At least not compared to where you come from."

"I'm looking forward to it," I said, stealing another glance.

She returned the schedule to me, then reached into the box and withdrew a trophy. "Holston High Math Olympiad," she said, reading the words etched into the brass plate at the bottom. "You're a mathlete?"

Why hadn't I pitched these before the move? "To be clear, I'm an athlete first," I said. "But yes, I do well in math and science. Does that surprise you?"

"No—I didn't mean it like that, it's just—"

"I think I get it from my dad. He was a navy pilot... smartest person I've ever met." I cleared a spot at the top of the dresser and arranged the trophies. "What about you? Let me guess, honor student?"

"Hardly," she admitted. "I do okay in school, but there's nothing I'm great at. But I like to read a lot. I've been reading at a college level since middle school."

I could tell she wanted to smile, but she held back. Perhaps she thought she was sparing me from the embarrassment of emasculation, but I had been told the same thing when I was in fifth grade by Mrs. Mortenson. I didn't see how bringing that up now would have done me any favors, so I smiled and nodded instead. "Impressive. What do you like to read?"

"Fiction mostly. Like any girl, I'm a sucker for romance, but I also like mysteries and occasionally a good horror story. The classics are my favorite though—Chaucer, Dickens, Brontë." The glint returned to her eyes.

"Let me get this straight." I put another trophy in place and stepped back to admire my work. "You like comics... obviously know how to use a knife... and read horror stories? No offense, but you're more of a guy than some of the guys I know."

"Gee, thanks!" She folded her arms at her chest.

I could tell she was mildly offended, but that wasn't my intent. "No. It's not a bad thing. It's just—you're different from the girls back home."

"Um. Again, thanks."

I was really digging myself a hole now. "No. God, this is all coming out wrong. I mean different in a good way. Trust me."

"Better." She unfolded her arms and flashed a smile.

"Amanda Gertrude!" The sound of her mother's voice echoing up the stairs caught both of us off guard.

"Gertrude?" It was a name that should be reserved for someone five times her age.

"Don't ask. Coming mother!" She smiled. "Well, this was fun. My house next time, okay?" She batted her eyes at me as she turned for the door.

If she was going for alluring, it worked. I was sold on Amanda Davenport hook, line, and sinker.

CHAPTER

THREE

The week leading up to school went by in a flash. Despite being homesick, life was returning to normal, whatever that was. I spent those first few days unpacking, cleaning, replacing light bulbs, and fixing a couple of faulty outlets. I borrowed some tools from Mr. Freeman, our next-door neighbor, whose garage could have done double duty as a hardware store. Now that Dad wasn't around, most of the fixing fell to me. I didn't mind, though. For one, I was good at it. And I was hoping it would help my chances of getting a car.

All the boxes were unpacked except for a handful that contained some cookware and the ones labeled WINTER CLOTHES. Mom had me place them in the basement alongside some old paintings, a bag of stuffed animals from when I was a kid, and a pair of porcelain turtledoves Nana had given her for Christmas one year.

On Saturday, Amanda called around noon. She said she had something to show me and to put on some shoes I didn't

24

mind getting dirty. I grabbed an old pair of Nikes and met her on the front porch.

Behind my house, on the other side of the creek, lay a thick and dark forest. As we ducked into the trees, I felt as if we had exited Evergreen and entered an entirely new world. The height of the canopy above us was dizzying, so I kept my eyes on Amanda. Admittedly, it was difficult to focus on anything else. Her face was so painfully angelic, her movements graceful, like those of a dancer. She didn't walk; she glided. I wasn't at all nervous around her, which was puzzling after all the awkward encounters I'd had with girls back home.

"How do you like it here so far?" she asked as we strolled along the dirt path.

"It's still hard to believe this is my home now." I stepped over a turtle stopped in a puddle of sunlight to warm its shell. "Sometimes it feels like it's not real... like it's part of a dream. Honestly, it's not as bad as I thought though. It's just different."

"Different how?"

"Well, for starters, there are no mountains where I come from... and it's really humid here all the time... And these bugs..." I slapped at a mosquito as it landed on my arm.

"You don't have humidity in Rochester?" she asked, ignoring the murder of the innocent mosquito.

"Not like this. The wind blows off the lake most of the time, so even in the summer it stays cool."

"At least you'll get a tan here." She flashed a crooked smile.

My skin wasn't what I would call pale, but it certainly wasn't the golden honey color of hers. The last thing I needed was for her to think I had some sort of abnormality.

"I never really thanked you for helping me unpack the

other day," I said as we climbed over a fallen tree. "You didn't have to do that."

"You're welcome. Actually, I should probably be the one thanking you."

"Right—church camp," I recalled as we moved ahead. "Then allow me to at least thank you for being so friendly to me. To be honest, I didn't know what to expect when we moved here."

"Why?" she asked.

I shrugged. "Fear of the unknown, I guess. I've heard stories about how difficult it is for someone from the North to move South, and I wondered if I would be able to fit in."

We walked on for a few seconds in silence.

"I hope you don't think I'm crazy when I say this, but I feel like I've known you my whole life." Normally I kept comments like that to myself, but I felt compelled to say it.

"I don't think you're crazy at all." She brushed a strand of hair from her eyes. "Would it shock you if I said I felt the same way?"

I ventured a look in her direction.

"And don't worry about everybody else," she went on. "Once they get to know you, they'll accept you like one of their own."

At least one of us was optimistic.

"Think about it from their perspective," she added as we topped a small hill. "If I'm someone who's lived in Evergreen my whole life and one day a family comes in from New York, full of big city ideas and a crazy accent, what am I to think?"

Was she seriously lecturing me on accents? I shrugged.

"Let me put it this way. Most of them have probably been praying about it all week."

"Why?"

"They probably think Satan himself had a hand in bringing you here."

I laughed a little, but only because it sounded like the most ridiculous thing I had ever heard. "But my mom grew up here. That has to count for something, right?"

"True. But that was a long time ago. Besides, she's been in the *evil* North for so long she probably forgot to pass on her Christian upbringing to you and your sister. That's what they think, at least." She flashed another grin.

"And what do you think?" Her opinion was the only one I truly cared about.

"Honestly?" She flickered her eyes to me.

"And don't pull any punches."

We walked on a few more steps before she responded.

"I see two people inside you."

"Only two?" I chuckled.

"On the one hand, you have a good heart. I could tell the first time we met. But..." Her mood became somber. "There's a darker side to you—not evil, I don't think, but not good either."

Her words made the hairs on my neck prickle. I had never thought of myself as having a dark side. Still, I got angry a lot, especially since the funeral. My therapist said it was part of the grieving process.

"Is that all?" As soon as the words left my mouth, I wished I'd stopped while I was ahead.

"For now."

"Okay, now it's your turn."

"Me?"

"Yes. Same question." She seemed to be amused by this back and forth.

I searched my mind. I wasn't particularly good at thinking on my feet. "All right, I've got it." I settled on something that should be satisfactory. "I'm sure everyone says you're beautiful, so I won't start there." I glanced from the corner of my eye and caught her blushing, so I took a chance.

"In a vast sea of darkness, a star there appears,

Its light slays the darkness, assuaging my fears.

And in it lies beauty and leaves ne'er a doubt,

A star so bright it cannot be put out."

She stopped and looked at me. "Frost? No... Dickinson? No..."

"Mercer," I said.

She tilted her head quizzically to one side. "Wait, *you* wrote that?"

I nodded.

"Wow. It's beautiful."

"Thanks."

"I remember what it was like to be the new kid in town," she said after a minute.

"You mean you didn't grow up here?"

"You sound surprised? I moved here when I was ten." She picked up a maple leaf and tore at it with the ends of her fingers.

"Really? I would have never guessed."

"Why, because of my accent?" She had a playful smile on her face as she glanced over to gauge my reaction.

"I don't know. This place suits you, that's all."

She glanced in my direction but quickly looked away. "That's sweet of you to say."

"So where did you live before Evergreen?"

"Greenville, South Carolina. You heard of it?"

"Sorry." Geography wasn't my strongest subject.

"I'm sure it's nothing like New York." She chuckled. "But it's bigger than Evergreen. My parents both grew up there."

"Your dad seems like a decent guy. I saw him out working in the yard yesterday."

"Who, Ronnie? He's not my dad. Mama remarried when I was ten. Ronnie's great though, and he's good to my mom."

"If you don't mind me asking, where's your dad?" I hoped for her sake her situation wasn't as tragic as mine.

"Still in Greenville." Her smile faded.

"We don't have to talk about it if you don't want," I said, sensing some discomfort.

"It's okay." I watched as she tried unsuccessfully to conjure the smile again.

"You miss him, don't you?"

"It's not that. It's just... my dad isn't a nice person, that's all. That's why we left."

We walked ahead a few more steps, hopping over a tiny stream that was nothing more than a series of puddles tied together by a thin ribbon of water.

"You ever wonder what it would be like to be a tree?" she asked, raising her eyes to the sky.

I stopped and looked up, bemused. When I looked back at her, she was watching me expectantly.

"Oh." Her question was not rhetorical. "Can't say that I have."

"I think about things like that all the time," she said serenely. "You don't think I'm weird, do you?"

"Of course not." But the truth was, her question was peculiar.

We resumed our stroll. Up ahead, the trail veered right.

"It must be lonely." I finally settled on an answer that might befit the question. Again, not great at thinking on my feet.

"What?"

"The trees—they must get lonely." The right side of my brain was getting quite the workout, but I thought I was doing an adequate job of keeping up with her.

"Why do you say that?"

"I don't know. I just get the feeling this is a lonely place." Even though it was summer, beneath the trees it was damp and cool, which stood in stark contrast to the blazing sun and heat that existed beyond the forest.

"No one's ever answered it that way before." She studied my face carefully.

How many people had she asked? "What do you think?"

"I don't think the trees are lonely at all," she said. She looked up again and smiled. "In fact, I like to imagine them as one big family, all standing together, stretching their arms toward the sun. When the wind blows, if I close my eyes, I can hear them whispering to one another in a language only they understand." She paused. "Think about all the things they've seen over the years. Oh, to be one of them but for a day."

If I had stood there for a hundred years, I would have never thought about the trees the way she did. I was an analytical person, great at math and science, but beyond numbers and formulas, I was like a fish out of water. She went on about the trees for twenty minutes as we continued up the path. I had never heard anyone talk like her before.

When we came to the top of a hill, I saw the sun again. At the edge of the trees lay a flat rock ledge made of limestone. She led me over to it, and we looked out over miles of open country. I couldn't believe how high we were.

"You can see everything from here. Come on." She beckoned me forward.

"Thanks, but I'm fine where I'm at," I said as my legs turned to Jell-O.

"I won't take no for an answer."

I took hold of her hand. She was gentle and eased me out onto the overlook. Her eyes never left mine.

"Now," she said, "look down."

I must have seemed like a wild animal to her—untamed, waiting to be broken. Doing as she commanded, I saw the entire valley stretch out before us from Evergreen at one end to Grandfather Mountain at the other. I narrowed my eyes, and at the foot of the distant mountains, I saw the white rooster tail from a boat on Lake James as it glided effortlessly on the water. It was one of the most beautiful sights I had ever seen.

Completely mesmerized, I forgot where I was for a moment and moved closer to the edge. I felt her arm against my chest, letting me know I had gone far enough.

Amanda sat as close to the edge as was humanly possible without falling, letting her feet dangle precariously over the side. I enjoyed immensely being with her, but there was something about her reckless nature that frightened me.

"This is my favorite place in the entire world," she confessed, her eyes reflecting the brilliant colors before us like a mirror. "I bet you don't get views like this in Rochester."

"You're right." The only thing that would even come close

was the view of the Yacht Club and Lake Ontario from the Charlotte Genesee Lighthouse.

"There's our street." She pointed to a thin strip of gray that twisted like a serpent among the houses.

I followed it with my eyes. It took me a minute to orient myself, but I found the head of Old Lockwood Road and followed it up to the Bluff. I spotted her house first, then mine. They were familiar but different somehow from that angle.

"And there's the diner over there, and Milford's, and the library... and look, see the ball fields over by the river? I played softball there when I first moved here."

An athlete, I knew it. As if I needed another reason to like her.

"Where's the school?" The start of it was only two days away.

"There." She found it. "That shortcut I was telling you about is directly beneath us."

She was pointing at the trees below. I saw the creek from behind my house as it paralleled a path beginning at the school and ending up on the Bluff, a few houses down from mine. It was just as she had described.

I turned my attention back to the school. At such a distance, it wasn't an overly impressive building. From what I could tell, it was made of brick and had a flat black roof, and I could see the loop where the buses lined up in the mornings and afternoons. Behind it sat the sports complex, where there were baseball, softball, and football fields. I could see the word GIANTS painted in big green letters bordered with white in the end zones and a G at midfield. I liked the Giants—the New York version—and likely would have played football if not for my mom. She said it was too dangerous but permitted me to play hockey instead, as if that was the safer option. I had broken my forearm and lost a tooth by the age of ten.

Football season was just around the corner. Depending on how things went, I might catch a game, and perhaps I could find enough courage to ask Amanda to come with me.

———

WHEN IT WAS time for dinner, we descended the mountain and carved our initials in the side of a giant hemlock that sat at the edge of the overlook. She said it was to remind me of the time I conquered my fear of heights.

Even though I had only been in Evergreen a week, this was the best day yet. It surprised me how quickly I had forgotten about Rochester, and I had Amanda to thank for that. If everyone else in Evergreen was as nice as her, this was going to go much better than I had expected.

CHAPTER
FOUR

TRIALS AND TRIBULATIONS

When I woke Monday morning, my stomach was in knots. I wanted to take the bus, but Mom insisted on driving me. As if I needed another reason to be nervous. I tried to talk her out of it, but once she set her mind to something, that was it. There was little doubt where my stubbornness came from.

With a muted gray sky threatening rain, I grabbed a jacket from the hall closet and stuffed it into my bag. When we pulled up to the school, I jumped out the first chance I got. I couldn't risk anyone seeing my mom drop me off, especially at my age. Mom promised once we got settled, she'd use some of Dad's insurance money to get me a car. Given my mom's tendency to drag her feet, I wasn't holding my breath.

Under normal circumstances, the first day of school was an anxious experience, but because I was the new guy, there was a high probability of the day turning into a full-blown disaster. The good news, if there was any, was that I was starting at the beginning of the year. Otherwise, it would have been infinitely worse. I kept hoping I wouldn't be the only new student, but I realized the odds weren't in my favor. After all, Evergreen was the kind of place you ran from, not toward.

GOSSIP TRAVELS FASTER than the plague in a small town, and I suspected most of my peers already knew my story. That meant they also knew about my dad (Cindy Davenport had made sure of that, no doubt). I assumed she had already spread the word to the good Christian people of the White Hall Baptist Church, and they had all told their friends and family and so on and so forth. On the bright side, it absolved me from any long-winded and awkward explanations, so at least I had that going for me.

As I crossed the threshold to homeroom, I swallowed the lump in my throat, dropped my gaze, and slid past the first row of occupied seats. A pair of girls watched me with general curiosity as I hurried to the back of the room and slid into an open seat. So far, so good.

As the room filled, it was just as I expected: intelligent kids in the front, popular ones and bullies in the back, and the majority, who fell into what I liked to call social purgatory, sandwiched somewhere between. The second thing I noticed was that everyone here had tanned skin. I inherited my fair skin from my mother's side of the family, and I had dark brown hair, which didn't help my situation, but at least I didn't have freckles. I was an athlete, though, and had done a decent job of building solid legs from all the skating I had done, and my arms and chest weren't far behind, so I had that going for me.

"Good mornin'," came the voice of Dale Richardson, a heavyset middle-aged man with balding hair and glasses. As he shut the door and slapped his worn-out briefcase down on the desk, I thought about what Amanda had called him and smiled. "Y'all take your seats," he said with a thick Southern drawl.

Does anyone here talk normal?

As the bell rang, Mr. Richardson took up his clipboard and scanned the roster. Even from where I was sitting, I could see him checking the page from left to right, top to bottom. Suddenly, he stopped somewhere in the middle. I drew in a breath and prepared myself. Being new anywhere was uncomfortable, but it was worse in a small town. Most of these kids had probably been in school together since kindergarten. Like Amanda said, I was an outsider.

"I believe we have a new student with us today." An unnaturally broad smile worked up in the corners of his mouth. Why did teachers take such pleasure in this ritual of humiliation?

"Mr. Mercer?" He scanned the room until he found me.

Damn. The fair skin gave me away.

"Please stand, young man, and introduce yourself to the class."

I slid out of the seat without falling, which I considered an accomplishment given the number of backpacks littering the ground at my feet. I didn't have to worry about being red-faced because I was skilled at internalizing embarrassment. But standing in front of a room full of people I had never seen before made me slightly uncomfortable. I brushed the hair from my eyes as I swallowed the lump in my throat. I could feel the eye upon me, like thirty sets of daggers ready to slay me at the first sign of weakness.

"What do you want to know?" There's nothing quite as unsettling as hearing your own voice reverberate in a quiet room, especially when it's full of people. In the nanosecond it takes for the words to travel from your lips to your ear, something peculiar happens, as if the space itself shapes the sound.

"Just the basics," he said, eyes down as he jotted something on the roster. "Name... where you're from... a hobby..." He appeared to lose interest and might have forgotten the whole thing if I had pressed him, but I decided the reward wasn't worth the risk.

"Okay." This *should* be the easy part. I had rehearsed it in my head at least a hundred times over the weekend. "Hello. I'm Cole," I began with an involuntary wave. Instantly, I regretted doing so. "I'm from Rochester, New York, and I like hockey." The last bit of information had done the trick. Normally I would have stuck to name, rank, and serial number, but he insisted on a hobby. That was what they wanted—some juicy detail they could sink their teeth into. There was life in their eyes now.

"Ice ferry," someone said under their breath.

Why was there always someone who felt compelled to make a joke? My eyes darted to a worm of a guy, tall and skinny, who appeared as if he was the product of an incestuous relationship. Given my location, I couldn't rule it out.

Laughter broke the silence.

The theory about my inability to get red-faced was disproved as I felt a wave of heat wash over my face. I looked to Mr. Richardson with anticipation. Wasn't he going to come to my defense? Wasn't that his job? The teachers at my old school would not have tolerated such insensitivity and ignorance. Anger swelled inside me.

"Okay," said Mr. Richardson, only slightly successful at keeping his lips from curling into a smile. "So New York, huh?" he said quickly, which I assumed was for his own benefit. The laughter faded. "I had an Aunt Maurine who lived in Buffalo years ago, but I think she's dead now." He paused as his eyes drifted to the ceiling. "Anyway, what brings you to Evergreen, Cole?"

"My mom," I said, still somewhat miffed at his weak response and the fact that I was still standing. My legs were becoming weaker by the second. I felt like one of those animals at the zoo, on display for the entire world to see. "She grew up here." I hoped that would bring an end to the interrogation. Boy, was I wrong.

"My dad said she used to give the best hand jobs in town," said a fat kid named Lenny sitting a few seats away. How clever. I bet it took him all weekend to come up with that one. It appeared as if he had fallen from the top of the ugly tree and hit every branch on the way down. I almost felt sorry for him. Almost.

He gave an exuberant high-five to a sallow-faced kid sitting beside him named Jeffrey, who gave a blank stare, probably the result of his below-average IQ.

This time everyone laughed.

I looked at Mr. Richardson again. He covered his face with his hand to hide the smile. Fat ass.

I never really understood where the anger came from, as if it originated in some mysterious spring hidden deep within the soul. But at that moment, the source wasn't the issue because no matter the point of origin, it was coursing through my veins the way electricity does when you stick your finger into an outlet. When I was younger, I kept it bottled up so tight I thought I would explode, but that had been before my father slammed into the ground at five hundred miles per hour. Since that day, I saw no need for a filter, which landed me in hot water at my last school. I'd left poor Tanner Smith, someone I had known since kindergarten, bleeding at the foot of his locker, searching the crimson pool for the two white fragments of enamel otherwise known as his front teeth.

I shot Lenny a nasty look, the kind that said *take it back or else*, but he was either too stupid to notice or too brazen to care. Either way, it didn't matter. As I tossed around the idea of punching him right there in front of everyone, I couldn't help but think of the headline in tomorrow morning's paper —YANKEE TRANSPLANT ASSAULTS LOCAL BOY—PRAYERS AND CASSEROLES NEEDED. That'd be one I'd never live down, so instead, I thought about how the therapist told me to breathe whenever I felt myself getting angry. I tried that.

"Calm down, class," Mr. Richardson interjected, with more vigor now that the smile was gone. "Mr. Sanders, if I hear a comment like that out of you again, young man, you'll be in Mr. Dent's office so fast it'll make your head spin. Is that clear?"

"Yes, Mr. Richardson," muttered Lenny as he turned around in his seat.

Even at that angle, I could still see the rise in his round cheeks from the smile that was no doubt still stuck to his face.

"Thank you, Cole." Mr. Richardson motioned for me to return to my seat.

For the rest of homeroom, I didn't hear a word he said because I was busy staring a hole in the side of Lenny's oversized head. I knew nothing about him, but I already hated him and decided I would make him eat those words.

———————

BY THE TIME SCHOOL ENDED, I wanted to get as far away from Evergreen High and everyone in it as I could. I needed time to think, so instead of taking the bus, I took the shortcut through the woods—the one Amanda showed me. Half of me wished she were there, but the other half was glad I was alone because it gave me time to calm down.

Today had not gone according to plan, if there ever was one. And in fact, it was worse. It was bad enough being in a place I hated, but worse now that everyone thought I was less than a man because I played hockey. If they only knew. I would have loved nothing more than for them to lace up a pair of skates and meet me on the ice. Then we'd separate the men from the boys.

As I broke free of the trees and made the turn for home, I could see my mom standing in the doorway. The sight of her aroused my anger once more.

"I see you didn't take the bus," she said as I approached. "How was school?" By the stupidly optimistic grin on her face, I knew she wanted to hear how great things had been. But I was in no mood for chit-chat.

"Like everything else here, it sucked," I barked as I slid past her, heading for the kitchen.

"Cole, what have I told you about your language?"

"Save it, Mom." I dropped my bag in the living room. "I'm not in the mood." I crossed the threshold to the kitchen and moved across the parquet floor to the fridge. I got hungry when I was mad, and after the day I'd had, I was starving.

She trailed after me. "Not on the new carpet," she demanded. "What happened?"

"I don't want to talk about it, all right?" I said through gritted teeth. I tried to give her an out, to leave me alone before things escalated.

"No, not all right." She was unable or unwilling to take a hint. "I'm your mother and I want to know what happened."

I searched for a way out, but I was trapped. Which summed up my entire life. "I don't know," I shouted, turning on my heel. "Where do you want me to start? I mean, this whole thing sucks—pardon my language—the school, the town, all of it. Shit, these people don't even know how to talk right."

"Young man, that is about enough."

I knew that last curse word had done the trick, but I was too angry to care. The way I saw it, I swore in my head all the time, so saying it aloud was just the next logical step. A sin is a sin, at least that's what I had been taught in Sunday school, even in your head, and if I was already sinning, I might as well get the satisfaction that comes with it.

"Look." She tried to reason with me. "I know this is not an ideal situation, but I need you to work with me here."

"Not ideal? NOT IDEAL! That's the understatement of the century! This is the furthest thing from ideal I can think of." I reached into the fridge and grabbed a can of soda, then stole a pear from the basket and headed for my room as the anger swelled to critical mass.

"Stop right there!"

I froze on the stairs, summoning every ounce of strength I had to keep from going nuclear.

"You're not the only one this is hard on," she said. "I'm suffering too, and so is your sister."

I turned on my heel with fresh determination. She had pushed the wrong button. "She's five," I said through gritted teeth, pointing toward Tabitha's room. "She barely knows how to get herself dressed in the morning. And you—" I caught myself.

"What about me?"

I wanted to stop, pr maybe I didn't. Either way, I couldn't. There was only so much restraint in me.

"I heard you," I hissed. "The week before Dad died." I had been holding on to that detail for months, saving it for a moment such as this. I took a step in her direction. "You were talking to that lawyer. Were you planning on getting a divorce?" I grabbed both sides of the stair railing and leaned forward, towering over her in an overt attempt at intimidation.

A look of guilt washed across her small face.

"I bet you're glad he's dead!" My voice was low and harsh. I had never spoken to my mother with such venom, but it felt liberating. Perhaps Amanda was right about me having a dark side.

"Enough!" She recovered quickly from my verbal assault and pointed a shaky finger at me.

I flinched. There was nothing particularly frightening about my mother, except when she was angry.

"Your father and I were going through a rough patch," she admitted, her face pained. "But that doesn't mean I ever stopped loving him. I miss him so much that I can hardly pull myself out of bed in the morning. So don't you dare stand there and tell me I'm glad that he's dead. I'm your mother, goddammit, and you have no right to say that to me."

She was right. I had crossed the line, and I felt terrible for doing so. "I'm sorry." I descended to where she stood and threw my arms around her. She *was* my mother, after all, and I loved her dearly. But lately she felt more like an enemy than a friend. "I just had a terrible day," I said, easing the tension.

"I'm sorry, too." She wiped away the tears from her face. "But the first day is always the hardest. Tomorrow will be better. Trust me."

I did trust her, but I sometimes wondered if she forgot what it was like to be sixteen.

———

DESPITE ANOTHER RESTLESS NIGHT, the next day I awoke feeling marginally better. I was tired of being angry, so I decided to focus my energy on someone more deserving.

His name was Lenny Sanders, and from what I'd been told, he was the meanest guy in town. Surprise, surprise. He stood six two, weighted two hundred fifty pounds, and was built like a dump truck. On the surface, he appeared unstoppable, but the one thing I had learned about bullies, and people in general, was that everyone had a weakness. If I had any chance of getting the better of him, I would need to find his, and fast.

I finished my breakfast and headed out to catch the bus. Passing by Amanda's place, I noticed the lights were off, so I kept going. When I reached the bus stop, it was empty, but as I turned my head, I noticed Lenny and two others coming up the hill.

"Well, well, well." Lenny came up the street with two other boys gliding in his wake. "If it isn't our old pal, Hand Job."

One of the boys was taller than Lenny and skinny as a rail. His hair was red, and there must have been a million of freckles on his face. The other was short, stocky, and had a birthmark on the side of his neck that he tried to hide with the collar of his flannel cutoff. They didn't say a word... just stood there with stupid grins on their faces.

"This your stop too, huh?" Lenny smirked.

"It certainly looks that way, doesn't it?" I doubted Lenny was smart enough to pick up on my sarcasm.

"Lucky you."

Obviously not.

"I don't appreciate what you said in class yesterday about my mom," I said.

"Is that right? What are you gonna do about it, shithead?"

I hated guys like Lenny Sanders, but I was smart enough to know when I was outnumbered. I was nowhere near his size, but I was tough, and I had a temper. Unfortunately, I didn't have the reputation here that I had in Rochester, or Lenny would have thought twice about provoking me. Even with his size, the one thing he lacked was speed, and I had that in spades.

When it came to fighting, everything I knew I learned from my father. The two key lessons he taught me were: walk away whenever I had the chance but be prepared to stand and fight if I couldn't. The second lesson had only one rule—win at all costs. I didn't want to back down, but three against one were insurmountable odds, especially when one of them was the size of a house. Lenny alone weighed more than the other two combined.

Before things could escalate, Amanda appeared. She was wearing cutoff blue jean shorts, brown sandals, and a white shirt with lace on the sleeves. Her hair was down and glistened in the sunlight. She was like an angel the way she glided when she walked, and I was certain her feet never touched the ground.

"Hey, Lenny," she said with a smile and a wave as she passed by. The smell of lavender hung in the air.

"Hey, Amanda." He dropped the scowl. It was obvious he liked her. Who could blame him? "I didn't know you still rode the bus."

"Yep." She looked at me and winked.

THE BUS RIDE to school was mostly quiet. Lenny sat in the back, brooding. I was sure he had all sorts of insults to hurl my way, but with Amanda at my side, he was handcuffed.

We stepped off the bus and let Lenny and those two morons he called friends go ahead of us. "You like that asshole?" I asked incredulously, watching as he lumbered up the steps.

"Nah. I just thought you needed a little air cover."

"Thanks, but I can take care of myself." I didn't want her to think I was weak. She appeared to overlook my comment. "Has he always been like that?"

"You mean an a-hole?" She looked at me as we marched up the steps into the building. I wondered if she had ever said a swear word in her whole life. "Yeah, pretty much since I've known him, but what do you expect? He's only got his dad, and he's the same way. Like father like son, right."

We turned left and eased down the hall toward her homeroom. "What about his mom?"

"Bailed when he was five. She ran off with some guy from Charlotte, and no one's heard from her since."

It turned out Lenny and I had something in common. Go figure.

"Well, this is it." She came to a stop outside room 213. "Will I see you at lunch today?"

"I'll be there."

I MADE it through the first half of the day with no trouble. Thankfully, the only class I shared with Lenny was homeroom, and since I was technically no longer the new guy, I became yesterday's news. Lunch, however, was an altogether different proposition. Yesterday I had taken a temporary seat with a couple of guys from my chemistry class, but I knew it would be social suicide to make that my permanent home. No one outside of Amanda knew much about me, so I couldn't afford to have them thinking I was a nerd. Besides, there is a fine line between smart and nerd, and if you fell on the wrong side of that line, you risked becoming a social outcast.

I grabbed a tray and searched for Amanda, but unfortunately, her table was already full. Scanning the room, the clock in my head began to count down. I had only ten seconds to find a table. Otherwise, everyone would notice. Three... two... one... At the last second, I spied a table on the other side of the cafeteria near the salad bar. It had several open seats, which gave me pause, but I was out of time and options, so I cleared my expression and approached optimistically. By the looks of the three guys at the table, I didn't peg them as either popular or smart. They had Social Purgatory Club written all over them.

"Mind if I sit?"

"New guy, right?" one of them asked.

"Guilty as charged," I said.

"Have a seat, Yankee," said a Black kid named Jackson West. I recognized him from precalc.

I sat down and shook the miniature carton of milk. "What's up fellas?"

"Um, nothing," muttered a tall skinny guy with paler skin than mine. His name was Eugene Grymes. I could tell my presence irritated him. "Just trying to make it through another day here at the Rock."

The Rock—that's what they called Evergreen High, not because it resembled Alcatraz but because they had carved the foundation right out of the limestone. Eugene was the most miserable person I had ever met. I watched him for a while, tearing at pieces of white bread that lay in tatters on his plate.

"Who pissed in his Cheerios?" The intent of my question was twofold, to be serious and funny. I was at least half successful.

"Don't mind Eugene," said Gabe Evans, a stocky guy with short brown hair. He's still mad because his mom walked in on him last night while he was having inappropriate thoughts of Misty Greer."

A look of betrayal crossed Eugene's otherwise sullen face.

"You promised not to say anything," he whispered across the table at Gabe.

For Eugene's benefit, I figured I would spare him any further embarrassment and change the subject. Besides, I was still trying to decide how I was going to get back at Lenny. I wasn't quick to forgive and almost never forgot. I scanned the room and found him sitting with the same two guys from the bus stop, stuffing his face with pizza and fries.

"What do you guys know about Lenny Sanders?" I asked. "He seems like a real prick." I took a chance, assuming none of them were friends with that idiot.

"Please watch your language," squeaked Eugene, glaring up at me from under his lashes as he nibbled on a cracker.

Had I unknowingly said something offensive? It had happened before. I searched the faces of the other two. "Is he serious?"

They shrugged.

"Shit, I'm sorry man. I won't do it again," I said, my voice thick with malice. There was that dark side again.

Eugene was red-faced now. He gathered his tray and back-pack, stood, and left the table in a hurry. I had taken it too far, again, but I was still brimming with anger over what Lenny had said the day before.

"Oh, come on. I didn't mean it," I yelled after him. "Eugene." I surveyed the room to see if anyone had noticed. They hadn't. I bet no one ever noticed a guy like Eugene.

"Don't mind him," said Jackson. "His mom and dad have him wound tighter than shit."

Finally, someone who shared my affinity for swearing. It wasn't as if I went out of my way to do it, but it had a way of driving home a point. Besides, I never said anything too awful.

I had made a promise to myself to operate by the shit-damn-hell rule. Those were acceptable, and the occasional *bitch* or *bastard*, if the mood struck me, but everything else was off-limits, for now.

"One of these days he's going to come unraveled," added Jackson as he finished the last of his chips.

"Yeah, I just don't want to be around when it happens," said Gabe nervously.

"So, Yankee, we hear you live up on the Bluff?" asked Jackson.

"That's right. What about you guys?"

"Winston Street," said Gabe.

"Drexler Avenue," said Jackson.

The way they said it, I was sure they assumed I knew where they were talking about, and I probably should have. It wasn't as if Evergreen was a sprawling metropolis or anything. It had a dozen streets, tops. Still, I had only been in town a week and hadn't yet ventured beyond the school or the woods behind my house.

"How do you afford it up there on the Bluff anyway?" Gabe asked. "Almost everyone up there is a doctor or lawyer."

Jackson must have kicked him under the table because he jumped like he had been shot.

"What do you mean?"

"Well, I mean it's just you and your mom, right?"

I knew what Gabe meant, but I ignored it.

"And my sister," I added, then paused. "My grandfather left us some money a few years back." It was the first thing I could think of and not entirely a lie. He had left us a few thousand dollars when he passed, but the truth was Dad had a healthy insurance policy with the airline, so technically Mom never had to work again so long as we lived within our means.

"That's cool," said Jackson. "So what's it like up on the Bluff?"

"It's okay, but you can't beat the view." I glanced over my shoulder at Amanda. She was talking and smiling. My heart fluttered.

"Amanda Davenport," Jackson swooned. "That girl is all kinds of fine."

"I hate to break it to you, but she's dating Rusty Givens." Gabe chimed in.

Gabe's words hit me like a ton of bricks. "Who's Rusty Givens?" I spun around in my seat. It sounded like the name of a NASCAR driver.

"He's a senior." Gabe twisted the knife.

"And don't forget quarterback of the football team." Jackson piled on.

"Yeah, I was getting to that." Gabe seemed annoyed that Jackson had stolen his thunder.

"That's funny," I interrupted. "She mentioned nothing about Rusty when she was at my house last week." I wanted to mention our walk to the overlook but decided against it.

"Hold on." Jackson raised an eyebrow. "Amanda Davenport was at your house?"

I nodded.

"Holy shit! Dude, you're my hero." He high-fived me across the table.

"Swear to God. She came up to my room and helped me unpack my things."

"I'd like her to help me unpack my things, if you catch my drift," Jackson said.

"Yeah, Captain Obvious, we catch your drift," said Gabe, rolling his eyes.

"Hey, I know we just met, but you guys seem cool. You want to hang out at my place Friday night?"

"Us, on the Bluff?" asked Jackson, eyes wide. "I'm in."

"Me too," said Gabe.

"Awesome. My house, seven o'clock."

CHAPTER
FIVE

There was no one happier than me to hear the final bell on Friday afternoon, and although I had survived the first week, it was going to take a long time before I felt comfortable enough to call this place home.

I took the shortcut and helped Mom get the house in order, which wasn't difficult considering we hadn't had time to accumulate any junk yet. Mom and I were on better terms now, but I would have to work on my attitude if I wanted to keep things amenable between us. My motivation was almost entirely selfish as I had my sights set on a car. Some guys at school told me about a used lot over in Linville, and I was hoping to talk Mom into taking me, but I had to be strategic about it. She wasn't crazy about the idea of me driving in the first place, but I didn't want her to get too comfortable with the idea of me riding the bus every day.

As I put away the groceries, I recalled the good old days back in Rochester when Nathan and Max would come over and we'd stay up all night playing video games, reading comics, and eating pizza and Twinkies until we made ourselves sick. How I missed those times.

THE SUN WAS ALMOST GONE when Gabe and Jackson crested the hill on their bikes. By the looks of it, their luck with cars was as bad as mine. We ordered a couple of pizzas and grabbed a six-pack of sodas, then went to my room and locked the door. Mom had a reputation for barging in unannounced, which might have been all right when I was twelve but not now.

As we sat around swapping stories about cars and girls, my mind drifted to something I had thought a lot about since we moved in.

"I was wondering if you guys know who lives up on the mountain," I said.

"Where?" Gabe parted the drapes and peered out into the darkness.

"There," I pointed. Even from that distance, the flicker of light through the trees was visible.

"Probably Old Man Finch," said Jackson as he reached for another slice of pizza.

"Who?"

"Damn. I think you're right." Gabe withdrew from the window. "I'd almost forgotten about him. I take back what I said before, about living on the Bluff," he continued, turning to us. "No way would I have him in my backyard."

"Did you forget about Amanda Davenport?" Jackson looked at him as if he had lost his mind. "Damn. I'd brave a thousand of him to be on the same street as that girl."

Gabe grabbed a pillow from the bed and threw it at Jackson, hitting him in the face.

I felt like I was on the outside of an inside joke. "Who's Old Man Finch?"

"Only the meanest son of a bitch in Evergreen," muttered Gabe, eyeing Jackson as he prepared for a response to his attack.

"I second that." Jackson raised his soda in agreement.

"There used to be a bet if anyone could make it up to the old man's house and back, there'd be a crisp Benjamin waiting for them at the bottom," said Gabe.

"A hundred dollars? No way."

"Yeah, but that was before—" Gabe's mood darkened.

"Before what?"

Gabe was silent.

"Before the murders," Jackson said.

"He killed someone?" I asked.

"That's never been proven," Gabe said quickly.

"Technically, you're right," said Jackson. "But everyone knows it was him. People go up the mountain, but they never come down."

I rolled my eyes. "You guys are full of shit." I hoped they were, at least.

"Swear to God." Gabe held a hand to his heart.

"Ditto," added Jackson. He gulped his soda.

"And *everyone* knows about it?" My voice was thick with skepticism.

"Well..." They glanced sideways at each other.

"That's what I thought. You guys *are* full of shit!" I jumped up to get another soda.

"I'm serious," Gabe protested, grabbing my arm. "My

uncle Gentry was on the police force when it happened. To this day he swears the old man did it."

"Then why didn't they arrest him?"

"No evidence," said Gabe. "It wasn't for lack of trying though. They were on the mountain day and night for a month. You want to know what they found up there?"

"What?" I was completely captivated.

"Nothing. Not a bone, not a piece of clothing, nada. Even the dogs came up empty."

"Then maybe he didn't do it," I offered.

"Oh, he did it," said Jackson.

"How do you know? What if he's just an old man who wants to be left alone?"

"And what if he's an old man who's perfected the art of murder," Gabe suggested. "Either way, it would take a whole suitcase of hundred-dollar bills for me to think about going up there."

My eyes found the light once more through the opening in the drapes. I knew it was a remote possibility, but what if the stories were true? Maybe Evergreen wasn't as boring as I had initially thought.

A MONTH WENT by before I thought of the old man again, and it was only by sheer coincidence I thought of him at all. Before school one morning as I pulled a sweatshirt off the hanger in my closet, I knocked off a book from the top shelf. The *North American Book of Birds* was a holdover from the bookcase I had in my room when I was a kid. It had been years since I'd last laid eyes on it. The book fell open to page 113, and as if by fate, staring me dead in the face was a picture of an American goldfinch. My thoughts drifted back to the story Jackson and Gabe had told me, but I had since learned they had a reputation for twisting the truth, so I was skeptical of their allegations. I needed to hear it from someone honest, someone who wouldn't exaggerate the details. Luckily, I knew where to find such a person.

That I still didn't have a car was maddening, but neither did any of my friends, including Amanda. So Monday morning just after seven I waited for her to step out onto the porch before I left the house, then caught up with her halfway up the street.

Amanda had on a green sweatshirt and jeans, and her hair was up. I almost didn't recognize her. She was the best-dressed girl in school, but today she was slumming it like the rest of us. It made me like her even more. Even when she tried to look bad, she looked good.

"What's the hurry?" She turned to find me chasing after her.

"No hurry," I said, catching up. "I saw you come out of your house and thought I'd keep you company on the way to the stop. You don't mind, do you?"

She shook her head.

I wondered how far away she was from having her own car. If she got hers before me, perhaps I could ride with her to school instead of taking the bus and vice versa.

"I like the glasses, by the way."

"Really?" She pushed them up onto her nose. "I can see fine without them, but sometimes I use them for reading."

"They make you look studious." I chose my words carefully.

"Thanks." She flashed a smile.

My mood was bright. I hadn't talked with Amanda much since school started except on the bus. She had her friends, and I had, well, Gabe and Jackson. Besides, we only had one class together, gym, but Mr. Phelps divided the class, so the girls were on one side and the guys on the other. So apart from walking in together, there wasn't much of an opportunity to talk. To make matters worse, she spent Saturdays with her mother doing God knows what, and Sunday she was at church morning and evening, with a family dinner at her grandmother's place in Burnsville sandwiched in between. Her schedule exhausted even me.

"How have you been?" She tucked a strand of loose hair behind her ear.

"Good, but busy." I wondered if it sounded convincing. I didn't want her to think I had been ignoring her, but I wasn't exactly sure how to go about these things. We were neighbors, but I didn't want to be the guy who knocked on her door every day just to say hello. That would have been creepy. "Mom has me doing a lot of the repair work around the house—fixing outlets, repairing the porch swing—things like that. How have you been? I saw you and your mom out driving on Saturday. I waved, but I guess you didn't see me."

"I'm sorry. Where did you see us?" she asked as we descended the hill.

"In town. We were on our way back from Milford's. I needed some tools to put up a shelf in my sister's room."

"That's nice. I guess I don't recognize your mom's car yet." She frowned. "I'll commit it to memory so next time I can at least wave back."

"I've been meaning to ask you about that. What's with all the waves?"

She chuckled. "Just our way of being friendly. They don't do things like that in New York?"

"Sure, but not to be friendly. It's usually a one-finger wave, if you know what I mean."

"Oh. Oʜ!"

We walked on for a minute in silence. I was searching for the courage to ask her a question but had difficulty finding it.

"There's something I've been meaning to ask you." I finally forced the words out.

"Okay," she said cautiously. I could tell by the tone of her voice that my impending question concerned her.

"You ever notice the house up on the mountain?" I looked over my shoulder. It was hidden behind the trees now.

She breathed a sigh of relief. "You mean the Finch place?"

"Exactly." I knew she would know it. She was like a walking encyclopedia for all things Evergreen. "What can you tell me about it?"

"Why do you want to know about the Finch place?"

"Curious, I guess. At night I can see the light from the window in my room. I noticed it the first day we moved in and wondered why someone would want to live all the way up on the mountain instead of down here with the rest of us."

I heard her draw in a long breath as we neared the stop. A story was coming.

"I'm not saying I believe it." She turned toward me. "But they say the old man who lives up there murdered some kids a few years back."

Kids? Gabe and Jackson said nothing about kids. Part of me was sorry I asked.

"The story goes three teenagers got lost in the fog on their way from Linville to Evergreen. They stumbled upon Finch's place on the mountain and were never seen again. Legend is he buried them in the very spot where his garden now grows. No one's ever been able to prove it of course."

"So you don't believe it?"

"Nah," she said. "It's like most things around here, not nearly as sensational as people make them out to be."

"And what about the old man—Mr. Finch. Anyone ever seen him?"

"Mom and I ran into him at the store a few years ago. He was buying bread or milk or something trivial."

"What did he look like?" In my head was the image of a hulking figure with a weathered face, probably with a scar or a missing eye. Surely he had a reason to be mad at the world, a reason that would make him want to kill.

"Like every other old man I've ever seen. He appeared harmless to me."

Just when this town was getting interesting... At least she was honest.

The bus stop was empty when we got there except for Mrs. Milligan's golden retriever, Junior, who had followed us up the street. I searched for Lenny and the others, but they were nowhere to be found. Amanda appeared alarmed by their absence.

"I'm not complaining"—I scanned the area to make sure they weren't hiding behind a tree—"but does Lenny miss the bus often?"

"No," she said without hesitation. "He's here every morning, rain or shine."

I didn't give it much thought until we reached school. He

wasn't in homeroom either. And when I didn't see him in the cafeteria at lunch, I got worried.

Lenny wasn't at school the entire week, which meant something was terribly wrong. When the final bell rang on Friday afternoon, I took the shortcut through the woods to beat the bus, dug the telescope out of the box in the basement, and climbed the stairs as fast as I could. It was a birthday gift from Uncle Eric when I turned eleven. He was a cop and worked crazy hours, so I rarely saw him, but he always sent the best gifts.

Under normal circumstances, I would never have gone into Mom's room, but this was not normal. From what I gathered, Lenny was not the kind of person who missed school, not because he was at all interested in learning, but because he made it his life's mission to make everyone around him miserable. A guy like that doesn't take sick days.

From the window in Mom's room, I could see all the way to the bottom of the hill to James Street. It was the section of town known as the Flats. Not to be insensitive, but it was where most of the poorer folks lived.

Lenny's house, if you want to call it that, was on the other side of Hanley Creek, just beyond the bridge. It was attached to the garage where his dad worked on old cars. If I'm honest, it was more of a shack than a house.

I kicked out the legs of the tripod and pointed the telescope down the hill. My heart thumped furiously in my chest. It took a minute, but I finally got it focused. There wasn't a single light on in the whole place. I say that as if it were a sprawling mansion with many rooms, but the reality was it had five.

To satisfy my curiosity, I grabbed the BMX from the

garage, which I had outgrown two years earlier, and took off for the Flats. Mom and Tabitha were at the store, so I had time before they returned.

At the end of Old Lockwood Road, I took a right on Mallory Lane and followed it to the stop sign. I hung another right and found myself on James Street—that's where the Flats began. I had never been on that road, and as I passed the dilapidated old houses, I quickly realized why no one from school came down here. It was scary as hell—like a scene from *Halloween* or *A Nightmare on Elm Street*.

At the bend in the road just across the little bridge sat Herb's Garage. According to Jackson, Herb's had been *the* place to take your car if you needed any work done, but that was before Linville opened a state-of-the-art facility a few years ago. Now it took in a car or two a month from some loyal customers, but mostly its heyday had come and gone.

There was a small house attached to the garage where Lenny and his dad lived. The doors to the garage were open, the lights were on, and the hood was up on a hunter-green '76 Oldsmobile Cutlass. I had always liked those cars. I laid my bike down in the grass and crossed the yard to the front porch, trying to keep my courage up.

As if on cue, the door swung open.

"What do you want?" a man in a white tobacco-stained wifebeater asked in a gruff voice. He was middle-aged, big as a house, with a bald head, goatee, and permanent scowl. It all added up to Lenny's dad.

"Um, my name is Cole. I go to school with Lenny." My voice was shaky.

"Oh." His scowl loosened. "You're Marissa's boy, aren't you? I used to go to school with your mama. She's a nice girl."

I thought about that first day and Lenny's crude comment and wondered if his dad had really said it. Now that I looked at him, it wouldn't have surprised me.

"Y-yes sir." I don't know why I was having trouble finding the words. Maybe because he looked as if he would bash my head in at any moment. Even Lenny looked tiny next to him.

"What can I do you for?"

"I, um, was checking on Lenny." I tried to look around him, but he was so large he took up the entire doorway. "He wasn't at school this week and..." My voice fell off as he shifted, leaving a sliver of space for my eyes to examine the house. It was dimly lit, dirty, and smelled like bologna. I caught sight of Lenny standing at the top of the stairs. He wore a look of defeat.

"Yeah, he hasn't been feeling well." He glanced back over his shoulder and found him with his eyes. "He'll be back on Monday though; I promise you that."

His jaw was tightly clenched as if something I said or something he'd seen had angered him. I could see he wanted me to go away, so I thanked him and backed off the porch.

I turned and walked in a straight line to my bike, afraid to turn around and see if he was watching me. I got on my bike and pointed it back up James Street and was satisfied to ride straight back up the hill and forget about the whole thing. That is until I heard the screams.

On the other side of the bridge, when the house was out of sight, I pulled off the side of the road and laid down my bike in the weeds. I had always been good at spying, and I crept quietly through the tall grass and doubled back toward the house. I slid down the little piece of an embankment and carefully crossed Hanley Creek, trying not to fall in. Thank God it was still fall and the leaves were on the trees. Otherwise, I would have been completely exposed. From there, I caught sight of Lenny through the open window. He was backing up, hands in the air in a defensive position. It took a few long seconds for my mind to comprehend what I was seeing. Even from that distance, I could hear it, the sound of leather meeting flesh. A scream followed. For a second, I thought I had imagined the whole thing.

When the fog of confusion cleared, I crept out of the trees and moved stealthily toward the house. I was quick like a cat, and in no time, I had crossed the yard. Reaching the house, I could feel the splinters picking at the back of my shirt as I slid along the wall. Once I was at the window, I raised my head a little and found Lenny lying on the ground, holding his head in his hands. His father was tearing off through the living room in long, hulking strides. That's when I saw it—the belt he had wrapped around his right hand.

That son of a bitch. I hated Lenny, but this wasn't a fair fight. I was starting to understand why he was the way he was. I stayed by the window for another minute as I watched Lenny rise slowly to his feet. He held a hand to his head for a minute, then staggered up the stairs.

BY THE TIME I got home, my stomach was in knots. I was angry at myself for going down to the Flats. Now that I had seen it with my own eyes, I could no longer claim plausible deniability. Mom still wasn't back from the store, and I struggled with whether I should tell someone about what I had seen.

While I waited, I went to my room and tried to forget. I

wanted to push it out of my mind, but it lingered like a bad aftertaste, eating away at my very soul.

I ran back out of the house and went straight to Amanda's. She was levelheaded. She'd know what to do. I noticed her window was open, the white lace curtains fluttering in the evening breeze.

"Cole. Hey." She stepped out onto the porch before I could reach the door. She must have seen me coming. "You look upset."

Was it that obvious?

"Can we talk?"

"Sure." She closed the door behind her. "What's going on?"

"I need to tell you something, but you have to promise to keep it a secret."

"That sounds ominous." She folded her arms.

"Did you know Lenny's dad beats him?" Just saying the words sounded strange.

"Shh. Keep your voice down," she hissed as she turned back to make sure no one was listening. She grabbed me by the arm and pulled me to the side of the porch. By her reaction, I knew this wasn't the first time she'd heard this. "Where'd you hear that?" she snapped as her brow tightened in a straight line above her eyes.

"I didn't hear it," I said. "I saw it... with my own eyes." I took back my arm.

"When?" she pressed me, still with that look of determination.

"A half hour ago. I was worried, so I went to check on him. I saw his dad... and the belt."

Her eyes drifted away.

"It was sweet of you to check on him, Cole, but you should never have gone down there. I was afraid this was happening again." She looked off down the hill toward the Flats.

"Again?"

"Remember when school started, you asked me if Lenny had always been like he is?"

"Yeah," I said, thinking back.

"He and Kimberly were friends when they were kids. From what she told me, everything changed when his mom left town."

I could tell she was uncomfortable talking about it, either because she didn't want to or had been told not to. She looked back through the window now and then to make sure Ronnie wasn't eavesdropping.

"His dad started drinking a lot... I guess to forget about *her*," she continued, dropping her voice to a whisper. "The alcohol changed him, and he started taking out his frustrations on Lenny. The cops threw him in jail for a while, but that only made things worse. Then, a few years ago, it all stopped. Lenny started coming to school every day, doing his homework. I even saw his dad at church a couple of times. I was trying to help Lenny as much as I could, but Ronnie said it was best if I stay away from him. He didn't want me to get involved. He used to play football with Lenny's dad and said he was not a nice person."

"But you said things got better? What happened?"

"I think it all started again when school let out last summer. I saw him once with a black eye, but he told me it was from a fight he had been in with Tommy Rattner. He has a twin named Troy and they're both bad news, so I believed him."

"Who else knows about this?"

"Just a few people." She sounded ashamed.

"And no one does anything about it?"

"What *can* we do?" she said. "If you tell the police, Lenny gets hit. If you do nothing, Lenny gets hit. Either way, he ends up enduring his father's anger."

I understood the dilemma, but it did little to dissuade me from saying something. How could I live with myself if I sat on that information? What if next time it was worse?

"Well, I can't do nothing. I have to tell my mom." I hated Lenny, but no one should have to live in fear, especially in their own home.

"No, you can't!" She took me by the arms and gazed at me intensely. Her blue eyes had transformed into a steely gray. "Promise me, please."

I hated being stuck in the middle, but I agreed under the condition that if it happened again, I was going to say something.

"Thanks." Looking relieved, she leaned in and quickly kissed me on the cheek.

Our eyes met briefly as she withdrew. My mind raced, and my heart fluttered.

"I knew I could trust you." She flashed a smile.

"Amanda!" The sound of Ronnie's voice startled her.

"Coming," she yelled, releasing me. "You better get outta here, Cole," she whispered. "I'll see you later, okay?"

I slipped off the porch and watched between the rails as she went inside.

CHAPTER
SIX

MANY ARE CALLED

Monday morning, Lenny was back in school, just as his father had promised. But there was a knot on his head the size of a golf ball, and his left eye was the nastiest shade of purple I had ever seen. If he had been in a car accident, I wouldn't have known the difference, and I supposed in a way he had. After all, Carl Sanders was roughly the size of a Volkswagen, and his fist had collided with Lenny's head at over twenty miles per hour. Being a student of science, I knew that was akin to taking a fall from a two-story building. No one at school was brave enough to ask him about it though. Not even the teachers. But I didn't have to ask. I had seen it with my own eyes.

Amanda was avoiding me. She even had Ronnie drive her to school, which meant for the first time since school began, I rode the bus alone. Maybe she was afraid I'd bring up Lenny again, but I was a man of my word and had no intentions of breaking my promise.

What I had witnessed that afternoon at Lenny's was one

of the worst things I had ever seen. Still, the way I saw it, two good things had come from it: one, I did what I set out to do, which was find Lenny's weakness; and two, as a bonus, Amanda had kissed me, though I realized it was likely a bribe to keep me quiet. But who cares? Everyone has a price. Evidently, mine was a kiss from a beautiful girl. There are worse things.

Mr. Richardson stood at his desk, droning on with the morning announcements, but my mind was miles away. I took turns thinking about Lenny and Old Man Finch and had difficulty deciding which was worse, a father who beat his kid or an old man who could have been guilty of murder. In some ways, they were the same. As I had suspected for some time, Evergreen wasn't as spotless as the church marquee would have you believe, and there was something about the dark underbelly that intrigued me. Perhaps Amanda's assessment of my dark side was more accurate than I first realized.

"Mr. Mercer... MR. MERCER!" Descending from the daydream, I looked up and caught Mr. Richardson glaring at me over the top of his glasses. I supposed this was his attempt at anger—lips pursed, forehead crinkled, hands on the side of his hips. He looked like he was ready to scold me.

"What?" I asked in a voice mixed with confusion and irritation.

"The pledge." He pointed to the flag in the corner of the room, then turned over his hand, raised it slowly, and as if he had some magical powers, lifted me from my seat.

Everyone else was already standing at attention, right hands placed over their hearts. They were all waiting for me. If I was going to avoid uncomfortable situations like this in the future, I would need to keep the daydreaming to a minimum.

LATER THAT AFTERNOON, I stared out the window again as a light rain fell. At least I was home now, free from prying eyes. The story of Old Man Finch would not let go of my imagination. I thought of many strange things, such as had he done it? And if so, were the bodies really buried beneath his garden? Then I thought of something else. Even in a town as small as Evergreen, kids don't go missing without it making headlines, which meant that there had to be at least a newspaper article regarding their disappearance.

I phoned Gabe and Jackson and told them to meet me at the library at four.

They were waiting for me when I arrived.

"What's up, Yankee?" asked Jackson. "Still no car, huh?"

"Hey guys, and no," I answered, irritated that he kept bringing it up. "Mom said we might go looking next weekend if I do well on my history test." History wasn't my best subject.

The three of us hadn't hung out since that night at my house, but we ate lunch together every day, so I knew I could trust these guys.

"Why'd you ask us to meet you here?" inquired Gabe.

"I was thinking about what you guys told me about Old Man Finch."

"And?" said Jackson.

"I was hoping the library would have an old newspaper article about the disappearance of those kids from Linville."

"And this is how you want to spend your afternoon?" Jackson asked.

"I don't need any convincing," Gabe replied. "This beats the hell out of taking out the trash and washing the dishes."

From what he'd told us, Gabe had daily chores, which was like a prison sentence for a teenager.

"Good point." Jackson turned his eyes back to me. "Why the sudden interest?"

"Honestly? I'm bored," I admitted. "I need something to keep me from going stark raving mad."

"What about Amanda?" Jackson was always ribbing me about her.

"She's out with her mom this afternoon." I said the first thing that popped into my head. After all, I couldn't tell the truth.

"Well, who cares?" said Gabe. "Nothing like a good murder to spice things up. Am I right, guys?"

We went around him as we headed for the door.

The Herbert C. Rawlings public library was one of the nicest buildings in Evergreen. It had been around for forty years but had been kept in pristine condition, mostly from lack of use. Like most libraries, especially in a small town, it saw little action aside from folks like Darwin Hollister, the town historian, or Sandra McCabe, a lesser-known author. She mainly wrote about small Southern towns and the religion that held them together. Most of the kids in town used the library at the high school since it was closer, but it was small, and it never had the book I wanted.

The librarian, an older woman named Vivian Ray, pointed us to the back where the newspapers were kept. It was a small room with glass windows, which meant if we found anything of interest, we'd have to be discrete about it unless we wanted her to know what we were doing. We made up a story about a research paper, which she bought and said it delighted her to see young men our age so enthusiastic about education. If she only knew the truth, she would have driven us up to White Hall herself and made us confess all our sins before God.

The library had hard copies dating back two years. Anything before that was on microfilm, which went back another thirty years. If you needed anything earlier than that, you were SOL (shit out of luck) because a fire had destroyed it a decade earlier. Honestly, I was shocked at how much they *had*.

We spent an hour pouring through copies of the *Linville Gazette* and the *Evergreen Review* until we found one dated October 25, 1982. LOCAL TEENS GO MISSING—POLICE HUNT FOR POTENTIAL SERIAL KILLER, it said in big bold letters on the front page of the *Linville Gazette*. The *Review* had something similar. TEENS VANISH WITHOUT A TRACE—LARGEST MANHUNT IN COUNTY HISTORY INTENSIFIES.

"I think I found something." Jackson spun the papers around so we could see them.

"Shit!" shouted Gabe.

"Shh!" hissed the librarian from across the room, glowering at us as she looked up from her book.

"So it really happened?" I whispered incredulously. I was shocked and relieved at the same time. At least I knew there was some kernel of truth to the story. Now to tie it to the old man.

"Told you," Jackson said, looking vindicated.

"But it doesn't mention anything about Old Man Finch." I scanned the articles again. "What if it was someone else? It says here, 'Missing teenagers fifteen-year-old William Bender, his twin sister Samantha, and longtime friend Michael McNeely, all residents of Linville, were last seen on the night of Tuesday, October 22 as they departed Linville for the Fall Festival in Evergreen.'"

I looked up. "What's the Fall Festival?"

"What's the Fall Festival?" they repeated simultaneously. That they knew everything, and I knew nothing, was irritating.

"Think Christmas but bigger," said Gabe. "There are signs all over town. Haven't you seen them?"

I should have—would have—if I went into town. Honestly, I'd only been with Mom to the grocery store once and a couple of times to Milford's Supply, but that was only because I needed a hammer and some nails to put up a shelf and a couple of Einstein posters Mr. Jefferson had given me. Otherwise, I left the town stuff for Mom.

"Dude, you'll have to go with us," Gabe said. "It's down at the fairgrounds, over by the river. They have rides and games and..."

"Girls," said Jackson. "All the finest girls from school will be there." His eyebrows danced up and down.

"Sounds like the fair back home," I said. "But let's not get sidetracked. I want to focus on the murders... or disappearance... or whatever it is." It still wasn't clear.

"You had it right the first time." Gabe's mood was dark again.

"Then where are the bodies? You said it yourself. The police searched the mountain for two weeks and found nothing. What if they got lost in the woods and bears ate them or something?"

"Bears, really?" he answered, staring at me as if I had two heads.

"He may be on to something," Jackson said. "There are black bears around here."

"You're both crazy as hell." Gabe rolled his eyes.

Jackson fired back immediately. "Speak for yourself. My mom said she saw one digging in Mrs. Wilkins's trash last month. They're mean if provoked, especially if they have cubs around."

Gabe and I gave Jackson a funny look.

"What?" he asked defensively. "You think because I'm Black I don't know about stuff like that?"

"Look, it wasn't bears," declared Gabe, ignoring Jackson's last question. "Those kids were murdered. My uncle, the one I was telling you about, kept a scrapbook with all his notes in it. It's at my house somewhere if you guys want to see it."

"Hell yes," Jackson said enthusiastically. "Wait. How come you never told me about this scrapbook?"

Again Gabe ignored him.

———

WE LEFT the library at a quarter to five and followed Gabe back to his house. Jackson was right. Gabe's place wasn't anything to brag about, but I kept thinking it was exponentially better than any house in the Flats. We'd had an entire conversation about it at lunch one day. Gabe's place was in the center of Winston Street and was a three-bedroom, redbrick, single story with a cellar. It sat off the road at the end of a short driveway, surrounded by large trees. It was evident by the neatly manicured azaleas and rows of flowers out front that his mother took care of the place.

From what Gabe told us, it was just the two of them. He

said he never met his father and had no intentions of doing so, especially after the stories his mom had told him. To hear him tell it, his dad was a drunk and a womanizer and had moved to Florida when Gabe was five.

"Mom!" he yelled as he burst through the front door. He waited and listened. "Okay, come on." He turned back to us. "She's still at work."

We followed him down into the cellar. It was cold and damp, and the steps felt as if they would collapse at any moment. The smell nearly knocked me over. Gabe pulled the chain that lit a small bulb that swung back and forth until gravity brought it to rest.

"I know it's here somewhere." Gabe picked through a couple of boxes of Halloween decorations and one with Christmas lights, then came out with a leather-bound album, the kind you put pictures or awards in. He blew the dust off it, which made Jackson sneeze.

"This isn't your baby pictures again, is it?" Jackson took a step back. "Because if it is..."

"Funny," said Gabe. "What we have here, gentlemen, is the scrapbook my uncle kept during the investigation. Everything he didn't want in the evidence locker is in this notebook."

It surprised me Gabe had come up with something so helpful. The name Gentry Rhymer was printed inside the front cover and dated December 23, 1982, a couple of months after the teenagers went missing.

"Let me see that." Jackson snatched the album out of his hands. "Shit, look at this." He pointed to a lock of hair sandwiched between a newspaper clipping and the thin plastic film that held it in place. "Whose is this?"

Gabe craned his neck as he read the words scribbled in the margin. "Marlene Eberly."

"Who the hell is Marlene Eberly?" asked Jackson.

"Yo mama." Gabe grinned broadly.

"Why you son of a..." Jackson took a playful swing at him. I imagined they went on like this all the time.

"Kidding." Gabe laughed as he tried to defend himself. "Kidding."

"GABE?" The sound of his mom's voice froze all three of us where we stood.

"That's *yo* mama." Jackson chuckled and punched him in the shoulder when he wasn't looking.

"Are we in trouble or something?" I whispered.

"No, just give me a minute." Gabe winced, rubbing his shoulder.

Jackson and I stayed down in the cellar while Gabe went upstairs to smooth things over with his mom. I could hear the faint exchange of words, but the tone remained light, which told me we weren't in trouble. Gabe returned a minute later, looking relieved.

"Everything all right?" I asked as he appeared there at the bottom of the stairs.

"We're cool. Apparently, she knows your mom from high school or some shit."

I rolled my eyes. Why was I not surprised?

Jackson went back to the scrapbook. "All right. So what do we do with this?"

"It's too risky here. If my mom catches us, she'll flip out. She almost had a heart attack when my uncle gave it to me, and she only let me keep it because I agreed not to look at it until I was eighteen. We'll need to wait until she's not around." Gabe gave a look back at the stairs to make sure she wasn't spying on us. "How about tomorrow after school—the old fort behind the Alley?"

"Good idea, if it's still there," answered Jackson.

"What's the old fort?"

"Damn. Sorry. I keep forgetting you're not from around here." Gabe slapped me on the shoulder. "You know where Milford's is, right?"

"Yeah, I think I remember." I tried to picture it in my mind. I wasn't great with directions, but thankfully, the town was small.

"There's an old road that leads back to the train tracks, but no one's used it in twenty years. We call it the Alley. Meet us there tomorrow at four thirty, and don't be late."

I told them I would be there, then left so I would make it home in time for dinner, but not before introducing myself to Gabe's mom. I didn't want her to think I was sketchy. She was a pleasant lady, soft-spoken, and not in any way resembling the monster Gabe had described. She was of average height with long dark hair and brown eyes, and she was wearing a uniform from the furniture manufacturer she worked for in Linville. Gabe said she assembled arms for sofas and chairs. She said she knew my mom from high school, but she looked ten years older, at least. I supposed life was more demanding on folks here than it was on us.

I left Gabe's and bolted for home. As I raced up Old Lockwood Road, I glanced at my watch—6:02—shit! I was already late and was almost to the driveway when I heard a familiar voice calling out to me. I pushed down on the pedals and leaned back as the bike skidded to a stop in the middle of the street.

"Hey, Cole." Amanda ran out to greet me.

"Hey." I panted, nearly out of breath from the sprint. My legs were on fire.

"Um, I wanted to ask you something." She ran a hand nervously through her golden hair.

"I'm listening," I said, bringing my breathing under control.

She looked at me, then quickly dropped her gaze. It wasn't like her not to maintain eye contact. "I was wondering if you'd like to go with me to church on Sunday?"

Church? Did I hear her right? If it had been anyone else, I would have turned them down before they got the words out, but not her. If she'd asked me to go to hell and back, I think I would have said yes. I did, however, hesitate—only for a second, but it was long enough that she said if I was uncomfortable, I didn't have to go.

"Yes," I said finally and smiled. "I'll go with you. Besides, it might do me some good to get back into church." That last bit was for her benefit, and it appeared to work as it brought a smile to her face.

On my mom's side, my grandfather had been a minister, so we were in church almost every Sunday growing up. My dad, on the other hand, wasn't a very religious person. I think he had seen too many things during his time in the military that turned him against it. I was admittedly stuck somewhere in the middle. Good and evil existed—I was sure of that—and we were all capable of both. Then there was the whole God-versus-Satan, heaven-versus-hell argument, but in my mind, that still left more gray area that I hadn't quite got a handle on. But the way I figured it, I was only sixteen and had the rest of my life to work through those details.

"Great." She looked relieved as she retreated to the sidewalk. "Be here around nine. You can ride with us."

"Nine. Got it."

I watched her skip happily back to the porch and hoped she would look over her shoulder. I'd always heard that was a telltale sign a girl liked you. Unfortunately, she didn't look back.

Mom and Tabitha were already at the table by the time I parked the bike in the garage and made my way inside. They had started dinner without me. I told Mom the reason I was late was that Amanda had asked me to church on Sunday. I refrained from calling it a date for two reasons; one, going to church didn't feel like a date, and two, I didn't want my mom to overreact.

"That's wonderful," she beamed. "Maybe your sister and I could go with you." She cut her eyes to Tabitha.

Sometimes I wondered if this woman knew me at all. Did she think I would agree to that?

"No!" I looked across the dinner table at my sister, who was trying to hide the peas beneath her mountain of mashed potatoes. I turned back to my mother. "I mean... why don't I check it out first? If they handle snakes or speak in tongues or something, I wouldn't want it to scare Tabitha." I tried to sound convincing, using my sister as a pawn, but it was the first thing that came to mind. Deep down, I knew the chances of seeing something like snake handling were remote, but I was in the South, and I had heard plenty of stories from my grandfather about it. On the other hand, speaking in tongues was a near certainty, and to be honest, the thought of that was more frightening than the snakes.

"All right. But if you like it, we could all go next Sunday?"

"Sure." I sank into my chair.

That night and the whole next day, I was on cloud nine. The unimaginable had happened, and Amanda Davenport had asked me out—though if I thought about it long enough, I wasn't convinced it was her idea, at least not all of it. Something in her tone suggested her mom had been the inspiration behind it. Amanda was merely the messenger.

That made more sense. I could see Cindy plotting how to get my entire family in the doors of White Hall Baptist so they could indoctrinate us with their take on Christianity. I was cynical when it came to those things, but I was cursed to understand people's true intentions, and Cindy was as easy to read as a book. I had seen that the first time she set foot on our porch.

THE NEXT DAY, school was uneventful, so I came home, grabbed a snack, completed my math homework, then grabbed the bike and rode down to Milford's to meet Gabe and Jackson. Despite my terrible sense of direction, I only got lost once when I turned down Pennington Street instead of Bowright Avenue, but after running into a pack of dogs, I quickly realized my error and doubled back. Gabe and Jackson were there as promised. I glanced at my watch—4:28—two whole minutes to spare.

"You guys are early." I skidded my bike to a halt beside the old metal dumpster at the rear of the store.

"We just got here," said Gabe. I almost didn't recognize him with a ball cap on. "We might as well get started. It'll take a few minutes to get there."

At the back of the store, the concrete lot ended abruptly at the edge of a dense stretch of dimly lit woods. Over the past week, the sea of emerald that covered the forests around Evergreen had taken on hints of yellow. I could see the old road they told me about as it pressed off into the wooded abyss, hidden partially by the sea of shifting leaves.

Jackson went in first. Gabe and I followed.

We hiked fifteen minutes through the thick underbrush, ducking thorns and avoiding vines of poison oak that slithered up the trunks of trees like giant serpents. We turned left at a hollowed-out tree, then crossed a stream and climbed a small embankment. On the other side, the space widened, allowing fragments of late afternoon sunlight to reach the forest floor. At the outer edge of the open space stood an enormous beech tree with dozens of branches that writhed and twisted like a den of snakes. At the heart of it stood the fort, hidden inconspicuously twenty feet above the forest floor.

"Still looks like it's in good shape." Gabe examined it from the ground as we approached.

"I'm surprised." Jackson stared at it. "I figured those storms this summer would have finished it."

Jackson searched among the leaves and found a limb. He used it to snare the end of the rope ladder visible in the opening in the floor of the treehouse. He wrestled with it for a few seconds until it fell through the door and unfurled to the ground. Gabe went up first. He stuck his head inside and looked around, then gave us a thumbs-up. It was October, but the copperheads hadn't yet gone underground. The last thing any of us wanted was to get bit. The nearest hospital was in Asheville, and that was almost an hour away.

Jackson was second to climb the ladder, then me. When I

got inside, there was barely enough room for the three of us to work ourselves into a sitting position, and even then, our heads rested only inches below the ceiling. They had likely built it when they were six or seven. I imagined they would have had plenty of room back then. They said they constructed it out of boards they had gathered from an old barn torn down to make room for the ball fields. They had crudely nailed together and covered the boards with pieces of old posters and newspapers to fill the gaps. Small cutouts in each of the four walls served as windows so you could look out to the ground below in case anyone was around. It was impressive, even by my standards.

"Dude, how long has it been since we've been up here?" asked Jackson.

"A couple of years at least," said Gabe. "Probably the last snowstorm we had."

"Oh yeah. Now I remember. That was an epic snow battle."

The smiles lingered on their faces for several seconds as if the memory of that day was still vivid in their minds.

"So you guys don't make it out here much anymore?"

"Used to, when we were younger." Jackson's smile faded. "It somehow seemed much bigger back then."

"Oh shit, I almost forgot." Gabe twisted around and worked free a loose floorboard, then stuck his hand in the space and returned with a pack of Lucky Strikes.

"No way those are still good." Jackson grabbed one from the pack and the lighter from his pocket and tried to get it to burn, but it didn't work. "Damn. Waterlogged." He tossed it to the floor.

"Let's have a look at that scrapbook," I said before they

tried the cigarettes again. I wasn't keen on the idea of smoking, but I wasn't prepared to turn one down if they offered. I hadn't been there long enough to risk isolating myself from the only friends I had.

Gabe placed the scrapbook in the space between us and opened the front cover. He turned on the flashlight. It was still light outside but nearly dark inside the fort. "I think there may be a few things in here you guys might find interesting." He flipped the pages until he came to a place where the letters FF appeared with a circle around them.

"Fall Festival," I said reflexively.

"Yeah, that fits." Gabe looked stunned. "Shit, how did I miss that?"

"Way to go, shit for brains." Jackson rolled his eyes.

While they traded jabs, I noticed a name written in cursive near the bottom of the page. "Who's Neal Bonham?"

"Um, I think he runs Bonham Entertainment. They're responsible for all the rides and games at the festival." Gabe searched the rest of the page. "It says here my uncle interviewed him at the station shortly after the disappearance."

"Why would he interview the guy in charge of the carnival?" asked Jackson.

"Probably standard procedure." I had seen enough cop shows on TV to know about stuff like that.

My explanation appeared to satisfy him.

This back and forth went on for the better part of an hour as we built up theories only to shoot them down.

Gabe looked up suddenly. "Did you guys hear that?"

It was dark now. I looked at my watch—7:38. I couldn't believe we had been out there that long. My mind drifted to the bears Jackson had so eloquently told us about the day before.

"Kill the light," I murmured.

Gabe found the switch to the flashlight and flipped it off. We had been staring at the light for so long it took several minutes for our eyes to adjust to the depth of darkness around us. Our heightened sense of hearing made up for it.

There was a narrow opening in the wood planks behind me. I twisted my body into position and looked out, hoping to find anything but a bear.

"You guys see anything?" I hardly spoke above a whisper.

"Nothing," Jackson said.

"Wait." There was excitement in Gabe's voice. "Oh shit!"

I was sure it was a mountain lion or a bear. Knowing my luck, it was probably a wolf. Again, there were stories. Dear God, if it *was* a bear though... I was fast, but not that fast. Black bears could run as fast as a horse in short bursts, and if that wasn't bad enough, they could also climb. I sounded like Jackson now. Shit. We were in big trouble.

Instead of hearing growls or grunts, I heard voices, a pair of them. They were growing louder by the second, which meant they were close. Out of the darkness, two figures emerged, their slender silhouettes illuminated there in the silver moonlight. I couldn't be sure, but their voices didn't sound familiar, though it was hard to hear over the thumping of my heart. It relieved me it was not a wild animal, but that relief was short-lived.

"No way," whispered Jackson. It was apparent they knew something I didn't. Go figure.

"What?"

"The Rattner twins." Jackson turned to me with terror in his eyes.

I remembered the day on Amanda's porch and what she'd said about them being bad news. I wished I had made her elaborate.

"Is this the place?" I heard one of them say.

"I don't remember. Get the map," said the other.

"I thought you brought the map."

"Dammit, Tommy! You're about as reliable as a cheese-cloth condom."

"Shut up, you bastard."

They scuffled for a minute or two there in the moonlight, then disappeared back into the darkness, arguing the entire way. When they were gone, we descended from the fort and made our way back to Milford's. Luckily, the bikes were still there. We pedaled away as fast as our feet would carry us. I didn't understand why Gabe and Jackson were so frightened by the Rattners, but whatever the reason, it must have been a good one because I had never seen them fly on their bikes like they did that night.

AFTER THE CLOSE call the night before, I stayed home Saturday and passed the time playing video games, considering rain was predicted for most of the day. Sometimes it was good to have a day when you could lock yourself away from the world and not worry about anyone wanting anything from you. I hadn't had a day like that since we moved to Evergreen.

I had entertained the idea of calling Amanda, but while I was eating breakfast, I had seen her leave with her mom.

They'd probably be gone most of the day, as was their usual Saturday routine.

By Sunday morning, the rain was a distant memory, and the sky was clear again. One thing I'd noticed since living there, if you didn't like the weather, wait a half hour because it was likely to change.

My morning began earlier than I liked for a Sunday, a little after seven. When I agreed to go to church with Amanda, I had been so caught up in the moment it didn't cross my mind what I would wear. Mom helped me find my blue long-sleeved polo from the box of winter clothes, and she ironed it for me while I showered and combed my hair. I still had the yellow tie from my dad's funeral, so I did the best I could to work it into a Windsor knot before heading out the door.

"I think we match," said Amanda lightheartedly as I walked up the drive. She was wearing a navy-blue dress with tiny yellow daisies and a white knit sweater over the top. I looked down at my shirt and tie and noticed now that the knot was crooked. She walked up to me and adjusted it. "There. Perfect."

I was thinking the same thing. Our eyes met, but only for a moment. Then she looked away at the sound of her mother's voice.

"Look at the two of you." Cindy appeared on the porch with her camera and motioned for us to get closer so she could take our picture.

That confirmed it—this had most definitely been her idea. I tried not to let it bother me as I stood beside Amanda and tried my best to smile.

Ronnie appeared on the porch a second later and closed the door behind him. I had only spoken to him once but figured since he was good enough to give me a ride, I should go ahead and formally introduce myself.

"Good morning, sir." I nervously extended my hand.

Ronnie was of average height but broad shouldered and solid. He worked construction with the North Carolina Department of Transportation, laying asphalt on the highways. His hands were more like paws.

He glared at me through narrow slits in his eyes, kept me waiting for a few long seconds, then flashed a grin as I gulped. Evidently, he was satisfied his intimidation tactic had worked.

"Nice to finally meet you, Cole." His voice was deep, and he shook my hand in a vise grip. "Amanda's told us a lot about you."

That caught me off guard a bit.

"She tells me your grandfather was a preacher," he continued as we slid off toward the car.

"Yes sir, he was, but he died a few years ago."

"I'm sorry to hear that. Being a man of God, I'm sure he's in heaven with the angels watching over you."

"Yes sir, I'm sure he is," I replied politely, though I still wasn't sure of the whole heaven-and-hell conundrum. I slid into the back seat of their opal-blue '84 Chevy Lumina and shut the door.

The car ride was mostly quiet aside from Cindy blabbing about something she heard at the beauty salon the day before. Her perm was gone, and her hair was frosted now, which was a bolder look than the day we moved in, if that was possible.

Amanda and I made small talk, but it was slightly uncomfortable, especially since Cindy and Ronnie would lower their voices every time we made a sound. It was clear they were eavesdropping. It wasn't like on the bus or the walk to homeroom, where the conversation was free and easy. Here we had to be guarded.

The inside of the White Hall Baptist Church circa 1836 was exactly as I pictured it the first day we arrived. On the other side of the double doors, an older man in a suit was there to greet us, shaking our hands and handing us each a bulletin. Beyond him was a wide vestibule with a stone floor that looked as if it were hewn right out of the bedrock, and two doors on either side of a long window separated it from the main sanctuary. Inside were two columns of long oak pews, twenty rows deep. Upon them sat cream-colored hymnals that looked like they had been there since Cindy was a child, and there were two envelopes in the wooden slots on the back of the pews—one for tithing and the other for the Lottie Moon offering—to be taken up during the offertory hymn.

Down the center of the room was a wide, gently sloping aisle that ended abruptly in a set of steps that rose to a platform where the pulpit stood. Behind it sat two wooden chairs, one for the preacher and another for the choir director, and off to the sides sat the organ and piano, currently empty.

From where I stood, I could see the baptistery and beneath it several rows where I presumed the choir to sit. Overall, it wasn't much different from the church I had grown up in except it was much older.

"The Lord does work in mysterious ways." The voice came from an older woman with silver hair. She had on a long lilac dress with an orchid pinned near her left breast. It had gone out of style a decade earlier in New York, but I guessed it was brand new to her. She took my hand and held it in her own, laying the other on top of it.

"What a handsome young man," she said. Her eyes drifted

from me to Amanda. Amanda smiled politely, then flickered her eyes to me. I must have appeared nervous. "You're the spittin' image of your mama. I had her in Sunday school when she was just a little thing."

I nodded and smiled politely. Evidently, I was no longer a stranger in this town, which was both comforting and frightening at the same time.

"It's good to have you with us today, and tell your mama I said hello, will ya?" She released my hand, then nodded to Amanda as she joined a group of older women over by the door. I'm sure I would be the topic of conversation around the dinner table this very afternoon.

I said hello to several others before we proceeded down the aisle, stopping midway on the left side in what I presumed was their usual spot. Cindy sang in the choir, so it was Ronnie, Amanda, then me in that order on the pew. I set a hymnal beside me so no one would get too close.

I wasn't a fan of architecture per se, but when something beautiful caught my eye, I noticed. Each window that lined the sanctuary was made of stained glass and burned in brilliant hues of red, green, blue, orange, and yellow. I studied each one carefully as the organ played.

As the choir opened with "Shall We Gather at the River," I looked around the room to see if there was anyone I recognized. Kyle Jennings, a guy from my English class, was there, and Simon Bentley, my partner in dodge ball. I knew it was a long shot, but I hoped either Jackson or Gabe would be there, so at least I would get the satisfaction of showing them I was there with Amanda, but I didn't see them. There was one person, though, that I *was* shocked to see. In the back row on the right side, sitting alone, was Carl Sanders. I did a double take to make sure it was him.

I nudged Amanda lightly with my elbow to get her attention. She was singing dutifully, and her eyes were on her mother. She knew all the words. She leaned toward me, eyes fixed straight ahead.

"Lenny's dad," I whispered. After what I had seen, I couldn't be more shocked if Satan himself had taken up a seat in the sanctuary.

She looked over her shoulder, then turned back and nodded slowly, never missing a word. I couldn't believe she wasn't jumping out of her seat.

While they sang the offertory hymn and passed the collection plate around, I found an opportunity to press her about Carl.

"He's been a member here his whole life." She spoke from the side of her mouth. It was clear she didn't want Ronnie to hear her talking.

I didn't want to risk getting her in trouble, so I placed the five-dollar bill from my wallet on the plate and sat silently while the choir wrapped up.

Before the preacher took the pulpit, the choir dispersed, and Cindy came down and joined us. Amanda and Ronnie both told her how great she sounded, and she thanked them as she slid in alongside Ronnie. Amanda and I scooted down. Luckily, I had reserved an additional space because an old man and his wife had slid in at the end of the pew when I wasn't looking.

"Brothers and sisters," began the preacher in a lofty voice as his sermon commenced. His hands were outstretched, and his eyes were on heaven. "This is the day that the Lord hath made; we will rejoice..."

"And be glad in it," the congregation roared.

"Amen," he said enthusiastically. He opened his Bible to a place he had marked and stepped away from the podium, pacing slowly back and forth, hands locked. I assumed this was his regular routine.

His full name was Reverend Halbert Donald Ridgeway III, but everyone called him Reverend or Hal, depending on how well they knew him. He was a thin man, not tall, with jet-black hair and skin so dark it looked as if he'd spent his entire life under the sun. He had the voice of a Southern plantation owner and the ability to charm anyone with his silver tongue. He was a salesman through and through, which was helpful since he was peddling the most essential product of all—salvation. I watched with great curiosity the faces of both Amanda and Cindy; they nodded in unison as he finished every sentence, gave an *amen* even when it wasn't required, and appeared to be enraptured with every word that fell from his mouth. Ronnie, on the other hand, was expressionless. He was statuesque, eyes fixed dead ahead, moving only when the preacher moved. Maybe he was thinking the same thing I was, that this was all for show. It was difficult to tell.

I glanced back at Carl a few times. Once he caught me looking, I didn't look back again. He didn't appear quite as imposing in a suit and tie, though he still looked like an enormous man even from fifty feet away. I realized then that Lenny had not accompanied him. Knowing he liked Amanda as much as he did, I doubted he would have voluntarily missed a chance to gawk at her from the back row. I hoped he was all right.

When the service was over, I thought we'd go straight home, but instead, Ronnie drove us all over to Linville to eat at Wimbley's Diner. They had an all-you-can-eat buffet, and on Sundays, they had prime rib. Apparently it was Ronnie's favorite. We were Baptists, which meant we arrived for lunch a little later than everyone else, and when I say everyone else, I'm referring to the Methodists. I have to give it to them—they know how to get to the front of the line.

After lunch, we went home, and Amanda and I sat on the porch for a while and talked. She seemed different somehow, though I couldn't put my finger on it. Anyway, it was good to spend time with her again, and I didn't want it to end. But around three, her mom came out and said it was time for her to come inside and begin her chores, so we said our goodbyes and I went home, but that didn't stop me from thinking about her for the rest of the afternoon.

CHAPTER
SEVEN

CROSS TO BEAR

The Avery County Fall Festival had been on my mind for weeks. It was cooler the morning of the opening day, but I hardly noticed because the adrenaline coursing through my veins was enough to keep me warm. It had been almost a month since my "date" with Amanda, and though she had never called it that, I wasn't ready to give up hope just yet. I kept thinking she would invite me to church again or maybe somewhere better, like the diner or a football game, but surprisingly, she never did. Perhaps she was waiting for me to make the next move?

The more likely explanation was that Cindy had been behind the plot to get me into church. She probably thought I would enjoy it so much I would run home and tell my mother how great it was, and next time we'd all show up—me, Mom, and Tabitha, a perfect little family. What a story that would have made for the church newsletter—DECADES OF PRAYERS ANSWERED AS LOCAL GIRL RETURNS WITH FAMILY, STRENGTHENS

FLOCK. That would have been the jewel in the reverend's crown, converting a couple of city dwellers like my sister and me. The fact that we were from the North would have been icing on the cake, but it would take more than a few amens and hallelujahs to win me over.

My ability to read people, as I discovered, was limited to adults. They were predictable, set in their ways, and rarely deviated from their routines. Teenage girls, on the other hand, were an altogether different story. Most days, Amanda was a pleasure to be around. She was witty, charming, and made everyone around her feel better about themselves. But now and then, she was distant, and her mood seemed to change with the weather, which was often. I hadn't noticed it at first, but it was becoming a regular thing now that kept me guessing from day to day. Which Amanda was I going to get?

Despite our burgeoning relationship, there was still the lingering concern of Rusty Givens. I had seen him at school a few times and watched him compete once in a game I attended with Gabe and Jackson. He was a decent athlete but not anything to write home about, and although there was a rumor of him being offered a scholarship to NC State, I didn't think he had that kind of talent.

He didn't live on the Bluff. Of that I was sure, though where he resided remained a mystery, at least to me. He had already turned eighteen and looked every bit of twenty, and even though Gabe and Jackson swore he and Amanda were dating, I had never seen them together, not once, so at least I had that going for me.

I could have asked Kimberly or Rachel or one of her other close friends, but honestly, I didn't want to ask a question I wouldn't like the answer to. Fortunately, I had other things on my mind.

"I'll be at Gabe's tonight," I announced at breakfast. I filled a plate with eggs and bacon and shoveled it into my mouth as fast as I could. I ate a lot when the weather turned colder, and this morning I was hungry. Plus I was already late, and if I didn't eat fast, I would miss the bus. I rather enjoyed the ride to school now, sitting beside Amanda, and I didn't want to take a chance on someone else taking my spot.

My mother was really making a go of this whole domestic thing. Sheryl Bohannon, her hairdresser, had given her a recipe book and had even been over at the house a couple of times to show her how to use the mixer properly. We'd had these things in Rochester, but Dad did most of the cooking there, believe it or not, or we'd eat out, but Mom was making a genuine effort now. I admired that about her.

My mother was strong and smart; no one could dispute that. She had finished top of her business class at Penn, a story she often told, then got married, had a family, and balanced a successful career as a top-producing pharmaceutical sales rep. Honestly, I wasn't sure how she did it, and it had all come after she left Evergreen. As hard as moving to the country was for me, I realized it must have been equally challenging for her to move out of it. Until recently, I never really thought about things like that.

"Oh right," my mom replied as if she had forgotten. I knew better—she forgot nothing. Her mind was like a steel trap. "Are you guys going over to the Fall Festival? I hear it's going to be quite the shindig."

Shindig? Really? We didn't use words like that where I came from, and had it not been for Mr. Jefferson mentioning it the week before, I would not have known what she was talking about. Maybe it's true what they say about not taking the country out of the girl. I often wondered what my mom was like before she and Dad met. Maybe this was a glimpse of her former self.

"We might check it out," I said, thinly disguising my enthusiasm. "I'm sure it'll be lame, but..."

"Well, if you do go, just remember to be careful. There's always a story of teenagers going missing at these things, so stick together." It was as if she had read my mind. I wondered if she knew the story of the missing teens from Linville. A chill climbed my spine.

"I will," I promised.

I knew school would be difficult because my mind was already down at the fairgrounds. Amanda and I sat beside each other on the bus like usual and talked about Kimberly's birthday party, which was just a few weeks away. I had not received an invitation yet, but she assured me one was coming. I wasn't going to hold my breath. I had never received an invitation to a girl's party, but this place was different. The girls liked me here, and admittedly, I liked them right back.

When it came to Kimberly Davis, she and I had become decent friends since the start of school. She sat beside me in homeroom and had even added a spot for me at their lunch table. I'd sat with her and Amanda a few times, but usually I sat with Gabe, Jackson, a kid named Charlie Hammond, and the Shoffner twins, Eric and Scott—they were baseball players. But I had to be careful around Kimberly because our moms had a history. According to Kimberly, they were best friends in high school until Kimberly's mom stole my mom's boyfriend senior year. Evidently, it was quite the scandal. It was this stab in the back that finally prompted my mother to leave Evergreen after high school. I supposed, in a strange way, I owed Kimberly's mother my life since, without her betrayal, I may never have been born.

"So are you going to the festival? I hear it's going to be quite the shindig." The words sounded strange coming from me, and we both knew it. Amanda shot me a funny look.

"I haven't decided," she said. "Ronnie wants us to go to Raleigh for the weekend to visit his folks."

"But you have to go." I tried to avoid sounding totally desperate, but I really had no interest in attending if she wouldn't be there. I had already convinced myself to ask her today. There was no point in holding back any longer. Besides, if I really wanted to know if she and Rusty were dating, this would be the best way to find out. The only downside was being rejected.

"I want to. I've never missed one before, but it's all up to my mom. I take it you're going then?"

"With Jackson and Gabe," I answered. "I think the Shoffners and Charlie are going to meet us there." I gauged her reaction.

Out of nowhere, she started laughing, which was unnerving.

"What?"

"Sorry. I just have a really strange picture of you in my head right now."

That wasn't the reaction I was looking for.

She tried to gather herself, but whatever image was in her head must have been funny because a second later, she fell into a fit of laughter.

"Why don't we change the subject?" I asked, feeling both

annoyed and embarrassed. I looked around to make sure she hadn't attracted any unwanted attention.

"Sorry." She put her hand on my shoulder. "It's just I'm picturing you in jeans and a flannel with boots and a cowboy hat."

Well, that explained it. I could see it now, and I looked utterly ridiculous. Even I had to laugh.

"See?" she said, smiling.

I nodded. I wouldn't be caught dead in a cowboy hat—or boots, for that matter. "Wait. That's not the dress code, is it?"

"No, silly." Her laughter returned. "You can wear whatever you want. You know the entire town will be there, right?" She cleared her expression.

"I know, but the way Gabe described it, it's sounds a lot like the fair. We have those up North too, you know." The last part of that was likely a bit overdone, but it served its purpose.

"Oh, I didn't know. I'm sorry." She turned and looked out the window.

Okay, so it was overdone. Now she felt bad. That wasn't my intent.

We sat in silence for the next few minutes until the bus slowed to a stop in front of the school. We waited for the doors to open, then climbed out and headed for the entrance. Principal Dent was there to greet us. I still walked her to homeroom every morning, which had become part of my routine, but it dawned on me as I rounded the corner I was something of a lost puppy, tagging along behind her wherever she went. Did everyone else think the same?

"See you at lunch?" she asked.

"Maybe." I decided it was time to change tactics. After all, my wide-eyed, breathless approach to Amanda had yielded me a trip to church and a kiss on the cheek, which was more than most guys could say but not exactly what I was after. If I wanted to be with her, I would need to be more assertive.

Some students from the Beta Club and 4-H were spending the day at the fairgrounds, putting the finishing touches on the decorations for the festival, so there were more seats open than usual. I sat with Gabe and the others rather than the girls. I always felt like I had to be careful when I was around them because they were all best friends. It was like competing with an eight-headed monster.

"Look who decided to join us," Jackson joked as he kicked out the seat for me.

"Hey guys." I shrugged the backpack off my shoulders.

"All that estrogen getting to you?" asked Charlie. He was the tallest of all of us, almost six two, but his thin frame did not allow for any muscle. His brown eyes matched his hair, and his skin was russet-colored, likely a result of the one-eighth Cherokee blood coursing through his veins. He had to be the funniest person I had ever met.

"Something like that." I tossed a Tater Tot into my mouth.

"We're gonna meet you guys at the festival tonight." Eric looked up from his plate of Mexican surprise. He had blue-green eyes and sandy-blond hair, just like his brother. Unlike Charlie, they had no problem with muscles because they were in the weight room six days a week with the baseball team.

"We'll be there a little before seven," said Scott. "If you want to get on all the rides, you have to get there early."

These guys had a system that had been perfected over years of trial and error. Honestly, it was admirable. I was less interested in the rides, though, and more interested in whether Amanda was going.

I forwent the bus ride home and took the path through the woods. At least once a week, I ditched the bus, especially when I needed to think. It was amazing how quickly summer had given rise to fall, and now Evergreen was awash in orange and yellow. As I plodded along, the leaves floated down around me like giant snowflakes, covering the ground. I took a little longer traversing the woods today, mostly because I was thinking about Amanda but also because I had nowhere else to go. Gabe wasn't expecting us until after dinner, and Mom and Tabitha were in Linville seeing the doctor, so I had time to kill.

Briefly, I thought about walking up to the overlook. I hadn't been there since that first weekend, but quickly I recalled my fear of heights, so I nixed that idea. Instead, I wandered around in the trees for a while, thinking about Amanda and the festival and kicking myself for chickening out again. I wondered if I would ever have the guts to ask her out. Somewhere amid me being upset with myself and wondering if Amanda would be at the festival, I lost sight of the path and found myself lost in the woods. I looked around for something familiar, but the sea of trees and leaves all looked the same.

Then I felt the hair on my neck prickle, and I realized I wasn't alone. *Bear.* Why did I always think it was a bear? I turned around slowly and found the face of an old man glowering at me from under the brim of a hat. He was tall with leathery sable skin and dark eyes. In his hands, he carried an old shotgun, which was pointed directly at my head. Old Man Finch. My mind raced, and my heart, or what remained of it, did not beat for fear of making a sound that would tempt his trigger finger.

"Get off my property, boy!"

I froze where I stood and put my hands up in the defensive position. "I-I'm sorry." I found my voice.

He gripped the gun tightly in both hands for a few tense seconds, then released his grip and let the gun fall to his side. I drew in a breath to keep from passing out.

"Damn kids! Won't leave me alone for nothin'," he muttered as he scanned the trees.

"I-I wasn't trying to bother you, sir. I'm sorry. I was on my way home and got lost." I watched his eyes. They were on me again, sharp like a hawk. Maybe he was checking to see if I was lying. I forced myself not to look away.

"I know." He dropped his rigid countenance as he looked back at the woods once more, then turned with a grunt and started back up the hill.

"You're old m—I mean Mr. Finch, aren't you?" I was fortunate to catch myself. I didn't think he would appreciate me calling him *old man*.

He stopped. "You heard of me?"

I wasn't sure how to answer. On the one hand, I could deny it, but maybe he'd see through my lie; on the other, I could tell the truth, then what would he think? Would he assume I thought he was a murderer? I didn't want him thinking that, especially with the gun in his hand.

"I've heard *of* you," I said, choosing my words carefully.

He murmured something to himself. "You'd better be getting' home, boy." He was on the move again.

"Wait!"

He stopped and looked over his shoulder.

"Is that your place up on the mountain, the one with the light?" I asked bravely.

He nodded slowly.

"Can I see it?" My words sounded hollow there in the vast space of the forest. If I could make it to the top of the mountain, I'd be the town hero. That would impress Amanda and Lenny.

He thought about it for a few seconds, then waved me on as he resumed his march.

I followed him along a winding path that snaked its way up the side of the mountain that faced the town. As we ascended, I kept thinking what a terrible idea this was, but I pressed on.

On the top of the mountain was a clearing, and in its center sat a small house made of earth and wood. It looked much older than the houses on the Bluff. It was *his* house, the one I had wondered about every night since moving to Evergreen. I tried to look through the trees to see if I could spot my house, but it was difficult to make out anything through the camouflage of orange and green.

"Welcome to Spar Mountain," he announced as he stepped through a small iron gate.

"Nice place," I said, trying to be respectful, though if I was honest, it wasn't much to look at. It reminded me of my grandfather's cabin in the Catskills where he used to go when he needed to do some fishing or to get away from my grandma. I noticed he had a small garden of corn, beans, and squash, and at its center stood a weathered old scarecrow to keep the birds away. That was where the bodies were supposedly buried. I gulped. "I can see your house from my window." I don't know why I divulged that detail, but I suppose it had something to do with the fact that I was terrible at making small talk.

"You live on the Bluff?"

"How d'you know that?"

"It's the only place in Evergreen that has a view of my house."

He opened the front door and discarded the shotgun on the table in the kitchen.

"What's it like being up here all alone?"

"Peaceful."

He seemed to be a man of few words. I watched him shuffle his way over to a worn-out leather La-Z-Boy, ease down in it, and pull the handle to the footrest. It popped out like a jack-in-the-box. He let out a long sigh and leaned back. He must have been eighty, at least, though I wasn't especially gifted at guessing ages, especially in older people.

"Have a seat."

He offered me a spot on the green sofa in front of the TV. I did as he commanded. This wasn't so bad. Just like Amanda had said, everything had been sensationalized.

I looked around the living room and noticed the walls covered in a cream-colored wallpaper with tiny flowers. Above the TV were some old pictures of what I presumed was his family, and there were several plaques regarding his time in the military.

"You were in the service?"

"Yessir," he said proudly. "Army, Third Cavalry Regiment —World War I and II." Holy shit, this guy was the real deal.

"You were with Patton, weren't you?" Though I hoped he would overlook it, I wasn't quite as well-versed in the First World War.

"You know your history. I'm impressed. A lotta young bucks like yourself don't know a damn thang. Most times, they ain't got enough sense to get outta the rain, if you know what I mean."

"My father was a pilot in the navy," I explained. "He flew jets in Vietnam before going to work for the airlines."

"Most folks don't have no idea what it's like to serve." He looked me dead in the eye and straightened himself in the chair. "That medal there," he continued, pointing to a shadowbox on the wall. "I got that for the work I did in Germany. And that one—liberation of France."

Hearing him say the words sent a shiver up my spine. My dad would tell me stories about Vietnam when I was younger, but not the gory ones. He tried to keep everything as lighthearted as possible. I always wanted to hear more, but he'd always tell me I wasn't old enough to understand.

"In war, like in life, it's all about the sacrifice," Finch said philosophically.

"I'm sorry about being on your property earlier," I said.

"Been so long since I seen anyone. When I spotted you down there wanderin' around, I thought it had started again."

"It?"

He adjusted himself in the chair. "I suppose there's no point in ignorin' the elephant in the room. Most of the folks in Evergreen think I'm a murderer. I'm sure you've heard the stories." Thank God he had been the one to broach the subject. I was convinced there was no delicate way to weave murder into a conversation.

"Are you?" As long as we were being direct, I figured I might as well go straight for the jugular.

The old man chuckled. "What do you think?"

"No offense, but you look like an old man to me."

He chuckled again, louder this time. "You're right, I am an

old man, but that ain't what I asked ya." His mood shifted as he paused. "Perhaps we should start with somethin' easier." He laced his hands on his chest. "Do you think I'm capable of murder?"

There was something in the way he phrased it that was alarming. I'd seen a show on serial killers once, and I was struck by how they liked to toy with their prey. Maybe that's what he was doing to me.

"I think we all have the ability to kill... under the right conditions," I said tactfully. There, I'd said it, and it wasn't a lie. I thought all humans could do bad things, but most were never put in a position where they had to.

"I like your answer." He flashed a crooked smile. "Probably make a skilled politician someday."

"You like chess?" I tried to steer the conversation away from anything dangerous. I'd noticed the chess set when we first walked in. It was sitting on a table in the living room.

"Yes, I do," he said proudly, looking over his shoulder at the board. "My daddy taught me when I was just a little boy. You play?" He turned his eyes back to me.

I nodded. "My dad taught me as well. He always said chess was the ultimate thinking-man's game. Finite spaces, finite moves, infinite possibilities."

"Your daddy sounds like a wise man."

"Yes, he was." I dropped my eyes. "I suppose you already know. My dad died earlier this year—plane crash," I said solemnly.

"I'm afraid I didn't," he said. "I'm sorry to hear it. It's hard to lose the ones we love, ain't it?" He paused, and I nodded silently. "Have you got time for a game?"

I glanced at my watch. "Sure. Why not."

We went over to the table and sat down. It was the first time I noticed the rest of the house. It was like a museum. Trinkets and knickknacks were standing on tables and in curio cabinets, china in a cabinet on the sidewall, and a tiny oscillating fan in the kitchen that whined like it would go out at any moment. With all the breakables, any wrong move would likely have set off a chain reaction that would leave the whole place in pieces.

"Black or white?" he asked.

It surprised me he let me choose. There was something odd about a Black man asking me if I wanted to choose black or white. I wasn't exactly sure how to answer his question. The last thing I wanted was to offend him, especially with that shotgun nearby. After a few seconds and some deliberation, I settled on white, probably because I had always chosen white. In my comics, the good guys wore white. Black was the color of the enemy. I realize how ridiculous that sounds, but that's the way it was written. Besides, I knew white went first, and I liked to be on the offensive. *Defense doesn't win wars*—I'd heard my dad say it a thousand times.

"Very well." He turned the board around carefully so as not to disturb the pieces.

Everything was already set up as if the old man had been expecting me. I wondered how long the board had sat like that and also how his last opponent fared. I hoped and prayed it hadn't been one of those missing teenagers.

"White goes first," he directed.

"Well aware, but thanks." I didn't want him to think I didn't know what I was doing.

I pushed my pawn to e4 without thinking. My father had

taught me that opening move, and I used it 99 percent of the time.

The old man flickered his eyes to me, then back to the board. He wasted little time moving his pawn to e5, then looked up at me again.

The next few moves went rather quickly, and before long, the game took shape.

"You never answered my question," he said as I tried to concentrate.

"What?"

"Whether you think I'm a murderer."

I looked up as my blood ran cold. "I thought I answered." I straightened my knight.

"You said we're all capable, but you never said whether you thought I had."

"How would I know? I don't even know you."

"Fair enough." He paused. "How old are you? Sixteen? Seventeen?"

"I'll be seventeen in March," I said, trying to make myself sound older.

"I thought so. I was about your age when I joined the army."

Now that he had successfully broken my concentration, I looked up and sat back in the chair. It was clear this was part of his strategy.

"Because I wasn't eighteen yet, my mama and daddy wouldn't sign the papers, so I forged 'em. When I finally got around to tellin' Mama, she was devastated. I can't say Daddy was any happier, but at least he was proud. He had seen his fair share of action, so he knew what I was gettin' into."

I looked down at my watch.

"Shit!" It was already after six. I'd lost track of time. I looked up, realizing what I had said. "Sorry, Mr. Finch. I didn't mean to..."

"No need apologizin' to me, boy." He looked amused. "I ain't no saint, and trust me, I've done my fair share of swearin'. Hell, I cussed three times before breakfast this mornin'." He chuckled heartily.

"I'm afraid I need to be going. I told my friends I would meet them after dinner. We're going to the festival tonight."

"Well, you'd better be goin' then. It'll be dark soon, and these woods aren't the safest place to be when the sun goes down. Bears and such." His tone was dark and foreboding.

"Well, again, I'm sorry for being on your property. It won't happen again."

"Water under the bridge. You're welcome here anytime. Maybe you'll come back again so we can finish our game. I think it has genuine possibilities." He extended his hand, and I shook it immediately. I was still wary of him and didn't want to do anything to set him off.

"Um, yeah, I'd like that." I ducked out the door at half past six. The sun was sitting low in the sky. The old man's words played in my head as I descended the mountain. I got out of the woods as fast as possible and didn't look back until I was home.

I went in, grabbed a sandwich and a soda, then jumped on my bike and rode to Gabe's as fast as I could. I realized my backpack was still in the woods where I dropped it. I'd have to go by first thing in the morning and get it before school.

CHAPTER
EIGHT

Gabe was lying on the porch swing, staring up at the ceiling, when I arrived. He was too big for it, and his feet hung over the edge. Jackson was leaning against the screen door, whittling a stick with his pocketknife. I watched for a few seconds as the ribbons of wood fell and collected in a pile at his feet.

Even before I saw them, I could hear them arguing over who they thought might win homecoming queen, and as usual, they didn't agree. Gabe was sure it would be Marie Helton, but Jackson told him he was crazy as hell, and as far as he was concerned, it had to be Whitney Slover. They didn't ask my opinion, and I was glad because I knew better than both of them who the real winner should be, but Amanda wasn't into things like that.

"It's about time." Jackson closed the knife and stuffed it into his pocket. I could tell by the look on his face he was irritated.

"Where the hell have you been?" asked Gabe. He sat up so fast he paled. Once the blood flow returned to his brain, he stuck his head inside the door to let his mom know we were leaving.

"Sorry guys," I said, "but you're never going to believe where I've been."

"This better be good." Jackson stepped off the porch.

"Where's the one place in Evergreen no sane person would ever go?" I gave it a moment to sink in. I wanted to drag this out, for dramatic effect of course.

Gabe looked at me curiously, eyes narrowed, as he turned over the prospect of whether I had done it.

"You didn't?" he said. "Shit, you did! You were—"

"On the mountain."

"Holy shit!" they said at the same time.

"How... why...?" Jackson was having difficulty getting the words out.

"I'll tell you on the way." I turned my bike and pointed it toward town.

Gabe and Jackson forgot all about me being late and jumped on their bikes as we raced for the festival. The Avery County Fairgrounds were on the south side of Evergreen, a ten-minute ride from Winston Street if we hurried, so there was just enough time to relay to them the details of my encounter with Old Man Finch. When I was finished recounting for them all that had happened since school let out, neither of them couldn't believe I had survived to tell it.

"You're one lucky bastard." Jackson shook his head in disbelief. "If Old Man Finch had pointed that shotgun at me, I would have died right there."

"Not without shitting your pants first," added Gabe.

Jackson shot him a look of reproach.

"I think you guys may have misjudged Old Man Finch," I shouted above the whine of the tires as we raced down Corwyn Street. He was peculiar—there was no disputing that —and he had military experience, which meant he likely knew a dozen more ways to kill someone than we did, but nothing I saw had given me the impression he was a serial killer. Besides, from what I had seen on TV, you had to be severely twisted to want to kill for pleasure. That distinction was reserved for guys like Berkowitz, Gacy, and Bundy, and from what I could tell, Old Man Finch didn't exactly fit the profile. Plus he was old. By my calculations, I put him some- where between eighty-four and eighty-six, give or take a year. On the other hand, he had that shotgun, so I guess technically it was possible.

"That's what he wants you to think." Gabe's eyes were on the road as our bikes flew across the railroad tracks. "Old Man Finch is one crafty son of a bitch."

"What do you think?" I asked Jackson, finding him gliding along my left side.

"I'm with Gabe on this one," he confessed. "The way I see it, you're either the bravest person I've ever met or the dumbest."

Convincing them was going to be more difficult than I thought.

It was dark by the time the fairgrounds came into view, but the lights from the festival produced a glow that swelled far beyond the trees. The music grew louder, and the smell of all things fried reached us well before we got to the gate.

Percy Goins Park sat at the lowest spot in town where Hanley Creek poured into the Calloway River, the entrance road flanked on either side by two ponds. The first thing I spotted was the Ferris Wheel, with its red and green flashing lights towering above the trees. We dropped our bikes alongside the others below the oak tree and hurried to the back of the line. It wasn't as crowded as I had expected.

"There she is." Gabe pointed at a disk-shaped ride that spun so fast I felt dizzy just watching it. "The Gravitron had me so messed up last year I threw up all over Wendy Gilchrist," he said, looking as though he was proud of it.

"Shit. I forgot all about that." Jackson laughed. "She was pissed at you for like six months."

"Still is. What's your favorite?" Gabe turned his attention to me.

Back home, the fair came to town in August before the weather turned cool. It had all the traditional stuff you'd expect but also the Tilt-a-Whirl, bumper cars, a roller coaster, and the Scrambler. My favorite was the Speed Demon, primarily because it didn't involve heights.

"Not a huge fan of rides, but you go ahead. I think I'm going to walking around for a while. Maybe I'll run into Eric or Charlie." I didn't want to tell them the real reason I wanted to check out the crowd, but maybe they already knew.

Once we'd paid our money and our hands were stamped, we pushed through the gate and made our way to the outdoor arena where they were showing horses. Sam Kohler, a guy from school, had entered two of his Tennessee Walkers and was expected to win. His family owned a small farm on the outskirts of town. We stayed there for a few minutes, discussing our plan of attack.

Jackson was complaining about not having eaten dinner.

Neither had I, so we decided before we could do anything, we needed to eat.

Food trucks were lined up in a row between the pavilion and the swings. There was already a line waiting for barbecue, so we went to the next and took our place in line behind Mr. Kiesler, our American history teacher.

We went over to the pavilion and sat down under the lights at one of the long tables.

"You guys come to this every year?"

"Since I was five," said Jackson.

"Four for me," said Gabe.

"One-upper." Jackson shot him a look as he inhaled a piece of funnel cake.

"You have anything like this in New York?" asked Gabe.

"The fair comes to town every year, just before school starts. It's similar to this." I didn't want to go on about how much better the fair in Rochester was, but this wasn't bad for a small town.

"Done," announced Jackson as if it were a contest.

"Me too." Gabe finished the last of his kettle corn.

I was still working on the pretzel with cheese, so I told them to go on and I would catch up.

Gabe and Jackson disappeared into the throng of people as I finished the last bite of pretzel and washed it down with a swig of Coke. That's when I heard a familiar voice.

"Hey stranger."

I turned to find Kimberly Davis standing there. She was wearing jeans, a bright pink top, and a white jacket. Her hair was wavy and looked as if she had used an entire bottle of hairspray. Out of instinct, I looked to see if Amanda was with her. There was rarely a time when they weren't together.

"Hey Kimberly." I tried my best to hide my disappointment. "You here alone?"

"No. Rachel and Sara are around here somewhere." She scanned the crowd with her eyes. "Mind if I sit?"

"Sorry. Where are my manners?" I offered her the spot beside me.

"Such a gentleman," she proclaimed with a smile as I wiped the crumbs off the seat beside me. "How do you like it so far?"

"It's fine." *It would be better if Amanda were here.*

"You gonna to take a turn on the Ferris Wheel?"

"Probably not. Rides aren't really my thing."

"Come on, scaredy-cat. Everyone rides the Ferris Wheel. You can see the entire town from up there."

I had little experience in this area, but I suspected Kimberly was coming on to me. Recently, she had been paying more attention to me than usual—laughing at all my jokes, asking me to sit with her at lunch—things like that. She was a nice girl, and I liked her as a friend, but as foolish as it might seem, I had my sights set on someone else.

Seeing that she would not drop it, I agreed to one ride with Kimberly, but it had to be anything other than the Ferris Wheel. I was convinced nothing short of Jesus himself could get me on that death trap, and even then, it would likely take a great deal of persuasion.

We rode the Tilt-a-Whirl twice, only because the ride operator couldn't get the bar to release the first time. When we got off the ride, we were both dizzy and had to hold on to the rail for several minutes until the world stopped spinning. By then, Rachel and Sara had found us. They grabbed Kimberly, and the three of them took off for the Ferris Wheel as I set out to find Amanda. Kimberly seemed pleased, and so was I, figuring I had done my good deed for the evening.

I started at the pavilion and worked my way down toward the House of Mirrors, stopping once at the Duck Pond to win a stuffed animal. I knew Amanda's favorite color was purple, and I had my eye on a bear as big as my sister. After a few unsuccessful tries, I set off for the shooting gallery. I was good at that, so I figured I had better than even odds of winning something.

As I fought my way through the crowd, I glimpsed something genuinely devastating. It took a few seconds for my brain to comprehend and a few more for my heart to absorb the blow. Amanda *was* there. She was wearing jeans and boots and had on a green-and-black flannel shirt, tied in a knot on the side. I started toward her, but something stopped me, and I was glad it did.

Appearing beside her, leaning in for a kiss, was Rusty Givens. Defeat didn't describe it. *Thank God I didn't win that bear* kept running through my mind. I hadn't been "Pearl Harbored" like that since my dad died. I should have listened to Jackson and Gabe. I hated when they were right.

I wondered if that conversation on the bus this morning was just a way to throw me off the scent? There was never any trip to Raleigh, or if there was, she certainly had no intentions of going. It was the worst moment since I'd moved to Evergreen, and I regretted Old Man Finch not shooting me when he had the chance. At least it would have saved me from the unbearable agony of a broken heart. There was nothing I could do but turn away.

As if on cue, Jackson and Gabe appeared. What great timing they had.

"Sorry, man." Jackson slapped me on the shoulder.

"Forget about it." Gabe did the same.

I tried my best not to think of it the rest of the night, but it was hard since everywhere we went, they were there. It was as if they were following me just to rub it in. I kept my distance though because I didn't want to have to talk to either of them.

An evening that had begun with such promise had quickly spiraled out of control. To make things worse, Lenny and his pals were there, and they were looking for trouble.

"Guys, look." I pointed off toward the swings.

Even from that distance, I could tell trouble was brewing.

"Is that...?"

Eugene Grymes, the guy I drove from the lunchroom on my second day, was hovering six inches off the ground, and it wasn't because of some newfound superpower. He was at the business end of Lenny's club of an arm, another in a long list of victims tortured over the years. Eugene's face was red, turning redder by the second.

For a minute, we all just stood there in disbelief. Lenny had the strength of two men when he wasn't angry, but when he was enraged, he became something of a monster.

"Are we just going to stand here and watch this?" I asked.

Gabe and Jackson didn't respond.

"Put him down, Sanders!" I shouted, seeing that no one else was going to come to Eugene's defense. Gabe and Jackson eased away from me.

Lenny swiveled his eyes to me. It had been a month since the incident with his dad, and yet the knot remained. All he needed was a couple of bolts sticking from the sides of his neck, and his transformation into Frankenstein would be complete.

"What did you say, Hand Job?"

I hated when he called me that.

"I said..." My eyes scanned the crowd. Some were shaking their heads as if the end was near for me. "Put him down."

I didn't care about Lenny's strength or his size. I had two things going for me—speed and anger—and after what I'd seen earlier, I knew I had rage to spare. I was tired of Lenny dominating everyone around him, including me. I decided it would end one way or the other, right here, right now, in the middle of the Fall Festival with the entire town watching.

"You've got guts, Mercer. I'll give you that." Lenny let go of Eugene, who fell to the ground in a heap. Derek and Ricky fell in line and skulked behind Lenny with wicked smiles plastered to their otherwise ignorant faces.

"You really want to do this?"

"Do what? We're just gonna have a little fun with you, that's all."

"It'll take more than you and those two morons." Somewhere deep down, I hoped Jackson and Gabe would come to my defense, but they were nowhere to be found.

At that moment, I wanted to tell everyone how Lenny had gotten that knot on his head, but then I remembered the promise I had made to Amanda. But after thinking about it a little longer, I wondered why I even cared what she thought. What she had done was ten times worse than anything Lenny or those other two assholes could do.

"Why don't you tell everyone how you got that knot on your head?" As soon as the words left my lips, I knew I had overstepped, but I didn't care.

Lenny looked stunned. "What?" He looked angrier by the second.

"That's right. Why don't you tell them how your dad beat the shit out of you and how you cried like a little bitch?"

That was a little too much, even for me. The rage grew in his eyes. They were black as the night. The crowd continued to swell around us, some pointing and laughing. We were standing in a bit of a corridor, a wall of people on both sides. I could hear them talking about the fight that was undoubtedly about to ensue.

Lenny took a step back and surveyed the crowd. It was too late now for either of us to walk away. Our reputations were on the line, so we were in it up to our eyeballs no matter the outcome. He bent over the way a linebacker would, in a three-point stance, and without warning, charged straight at me. The space was wide, but he took up at least half of it.

My brain was working overtime. I stepped to the side at the last possible second, like a matador, as he slid by uneventfully. He looked bewildered, unsure of why his shoulder hadn't found my rib cage. He turned back, angrier, and charged once more. Again I evaded him.

"Stay still, Hand Job," he growled.

But now everyone was cheering me on. They found it amusing to watch Lenny grab at the air like the dumb ogre he was. Apparently, it was the first time anyone had stood up to him. I was holding my own, but even I knew I couldn't dodge him all night. Eventually, when push came to shove, someone was going to bleed.

"Hit him, Lenny," I heard Derek say.

"Kick the shit out of him," urged Ricky.

Their voices sounded even more ignorant when they were excited, but no one else seemed to notice.

After another pass, Derek and Ricky stepped forward and

joined the fray, as if tired of seeing their friend look foolish. I looked over my shoulder and saw them charging from behind me. It all came together like the perfect storm: Lenny came from one direction, Derek and Ricky from another, and I was right in the middle.

My life flashed before my eyes in slow motion. I instinctively shifted to the side, and the three of them collided like a car crash, with arms and legs flailing about this way and that. The impact sent all three of them to the ground. To my surprise, Derek and Ricky were out cold. Lenny was awake but dazed, and oddly enough, he reminded me of a beetle on its back. I saw an opportunity.

I pounced on Lenny and drove my fist directly to the bridge of his nose. He let out a groan. I could feel the bone shatter under my fist, the blow casting a crimson mist on the guys standing beside us. I felt emboldened by the satisfaction that came with the contact and put the adrenaline to good use. Another fist came down, then another, and another, and before I knew it, the fat face of Lenny Sanders was a swelling and unrecognizable bloody mess.

If not for Deputy Irwin, a man who stood six three and weighed nearly as much as Lenny, I might have killed Lenny Sanders that night. Fortunately, for both of us, he jumped in and broke it up.

The crowd's shouts left me feeling ten feet tall as he led me off toward the pavilion. I had done it. I alone had defeated the giant. It must have been what David felt like against Goliath. It was the greatest moment of my life.

Officer Irwin drove me home, much to my chagrin, and as expected, my mother was furious. She disagreed with fighting under any circumstances and said I was grounded for a week.

I wished my dad were around; he would have understood. Still, it wasn't nearly as bad as what happened with Amanda. As Jackson later told me, she had been in the crowd and watched me beat Lenny to a pulp, convinced she had been right all along regarding my dark side.

I tried to tell my side of the story, but she wasn't taking my phone calls. I wondered how Rusty would have handled the situation. She might have had a soft spot for Lenny, but I didn't, and if she couldn't understand why I did what I did, then she would have to get over it or never talk to me again.

That night as I lay in bed, for the first time since moving to Evergreen, I felt like packing my things, sneaking out in the middle of the night, and catching a bus that would take me far away. After what I'd done to Lenny, I should have been satisfied, and at first, I was, but the longer I lingered on it, I felt ashamed that my anger had gotten the best of me.

Most of my misery had nothing to do with the fight itself and more to do with Amanda. She had been the reason I forgot Rochester so quickly and the reason I had given Evergreen a chance in the first place. But given what I had seen at the festival, it was clear she had no interest in me other than as a friend. In some ways, it was worse than the pain I felt when my dad died.

Most nights, sleep didn't come easy, but that night it was damn near impossible. So I sat at the end of the bed and stared out the window at Finch's place as I tried to push the image of Amanda and Rusty kissing out of my head. The lights at Finch's place were always on, which was both comforting and concerning. I wondered if he was studying the chessboard, pondering his next move. I know I was.

I lay back down on the pillow as my thoughts drifted to

Rusty Givens. He was an athlete, but he wasn't particularly gifted in the looks department, at least from my point of view, and he didn't have an ounce of intelligence. No one could debate that. They made an odd pair, he and Amanda; he the dumb jock, and she the most beautiful creature I had ever laid eyes on. Damn, why did she have to be so beautiful? And it wasn't just that. She was bright and creative, and I could have easily pictured her at home in New York City or Los Angeles on the cover of a magazine or walking the runway. If Rusty was her ticket out of Evergreen, she had severely underestimated herself. The truth was, she didn't need Rusty to escape Evergreen or anyone else for that matter, me included. She had what it took to leave this town on her own and never look back.

On the other hand, Rusty was destined to be the greeter at Walmart, wearing one of those vests with all the buttons. I could see it clearly if I closed my eyes. Rusty. *What kind of name is that anyway?* I lay there staring up at the ceiling. It was an adjective, something to describe the color of paint or a piece of metal left out in the rain too long. It also meant out of practice, which is how I would describe his skill on the field.

I could picture his parents, with names like Ron and Tina or Bill and Tammy, sharing a booth at Burger King just hours before delivery, trying their damnedest to come up with a name for their baby as they scarfed down a Whopper and fries. How the hell they not only landed on Rusty but decided it was the best of whatever they had come up with was beyond me. Only in the South.

CHAPTER
NINE

The Lion's Den

Cold is the worst, especially when you're out in it. Halloween was the dreariest night we'd had since moving to Evergreen. The cloud layer, which rolled in a little before sunset, was thick and accompanied by a howling wind. Finch's house was still visible though, shining like a lighthouse in the storm. Despite the gloominess, at least the rain was gone, so I felt marginally better.

I promised Jackson and Gabe I would walk the streets with them searching for a party, though from what I gathered, our odds of finding one were remote. It wasn't the same as when I was younger. I used to love Halloween; it was my favorite night of the year next to Christmas Eve. Back then, I would dress in my Iron Man costume and go door-to-door until my pillowcase was so heavy I'd have to return home, empty the content on the living room floor, then head out again. Now the greatest night of the year had been reduced to sneaking our way into a party and hoping no one noticed. Parties in this part of the world were primarily reserved for seniors. Amanda would be there with Rusty—I was sure of that—but peons like Jackson, Gabe, and myself, we would be on the outside looking in, literally. How thoroughly disappointing.

"Be back by eleven," my mom ordered without looking at me as I grabbed my coat and slid out the door. She was preoccupied with making last-minute adjustments to Tabitha's costume; she was going as a butterfly this year. I took advantage of the opportunity and quietly made my escape.

The lights of the town were barely visible. The fog had not yet made it all the way up to the Bluff, but it wouldn't be that way for long. It appeared like a ghost the way it hovered over the valley below. Was it terrible that I wished it would destroy the Flats like the spirit of Passover?

"You made it," said Gabe. He and Jackson were almost at the bottom of a bag of chips when I arrived.

"Where'd you get those?" The only thing I'd eaten for dinner was a cold piece of pepperoni pizza from the night before.

"From inside," said Gabe proudly. "You want some?"

I grabbed a handful of chips and stepped off the porch.

"So where are we going?"

"I heard about a party at the Masterson's," said Jackson. "I know Shane's sister, Melinda. She said she might sneak us in."

Shane Masterson was the running back on the football team and best friends with Rusty Givens. He was a smartass if there ever was one, and even though he and I had never spoken directly, I had seen him in action in the cafeteria, where his favorite pastime was berating freshman. A real winner, if you know what I mean.

"I just hope we don't see Lenny and those two idiots out

tonight," I said as we set off down Winston Street. Derek and Ricky were so dumb they made Lenny look like Einstein.

"We should be okay," said Gabe. "Especially after you kicked the shit out of Lenny."

He was right. Lenny hadn't said a word or even looked in my direction since that night. "Derek's out of town with his dad, and Ricky usually goes to his cousin's place for the weekend in Boone," Gabe went on. "Besides, the ones we really need to watch out for are the Rattner twins. They don't come to Evergreen that often, but when they do, there's always trouble."

"What's their story anyway; aren't they like twenty-three?"

"Twenty-four, I think," said Jackson. "Think Lenny, but worse."

Worse than Lenny—was that possible?

"They grew up downriver in a place called Norma," said Gabe.

"Never heard of it." It sounded like an odd name for a town.

"Think of it this way. Norma makes the Flats look like Rodeo Drive," said Gabe.

I was shocked he'd ever heard of Rodeo Drive.

At the end of Corwyn Street, we turned right onto Kesterman and followed it until the road dead-ended into woods. The lights were off at the Mastersons'. I glanced up the hill toward the mountain. It too was now hidden in the fog.

"What now, genius?" Gabe asked Jackson.

"Um, maybe try Llewelyn?" Jackson turned on his heel.

We had only gone a few steps when we heard it. It was hardly audible at first, but then it was there again, louder this time. It was a distinct sound, the kind that comes from bone meeting flesh. I was no stranger to it and looked down at my hand as I involuntarily made a fist.

"You guys hear that?" I turned around and pointed my flashlight into the darkness. "I think it's coming from in there."

"I didn't hear anything, did you?" Gabe gave Jackson a look suggesting he'd better agree.

"Um, no. Nothing," Jackson said. "Must be the wind or something." He smiled and said we should keep going.

They were lying. They didn't have an ounce of courage between the two of them.

Against their wishes, I pressed off toward the trees. I found a narrow path under the glow of my flashlight and followed it until I heard another thud. This time, it was close. I killed the light and listened. To my surprise, Gabe and Jackson were right on my heels. Perhaps they were braver than I thought.

I followed the sounds until I heard voices. It took only a second to realize it was the Rattners.

When I was close enough to smell them, I noticed something large tied to a tree. I moved to get a better look, and when I did, I realized the thing tied to the tree wasn't a thing at all. It was Lenny Sanders.

"Hey. Let him go!" I shouted, charging through the trees like a wild animal. I don't know why I said it, but I did. Sometimes my mind acted on its own before I could get control of it.

The twins looked up at once, surprised to see anyone out there at that time of night.

"Who's that?" One of them flashed the light in my direction. It settled on my face.

"Get out of here, Cole." Lenny looked up at me through the one eye he could see out of. He was a bloody mess and looked similar to how I had left him at the fairgrounds, maybe worse. Half of me delighted in his misery, but the other half—the good half—won out.

"Cole Mercer? I heard of you," said the taller one, though only by a smidgen. The ignorance in his voice was nauseating.

"Mercer, right," said the other. "You're the one with the dad that went..." He transformed his hand into an airplane and sent it toward the ground in a nosedive as he made a whistling sound with his mouth.

"Hey!" Gabe instinctively came to my defense.

"What'd you say, pork chop?" sneered the other as he took a step in our direction. He shined the light in Gabe's eyes.

"Come on man." Gabe tugged at my jacket as he took a step back. "Let's get out of here."

"You might want to listen to him," said the taller one, "before someone gets hurt."

I didn't scare easy, but I could see the shorter of the two with a hand in his pocket. He was hiding something. Before I could turn away, he pulled a knife and flashed it at us. The light from the flashlight danced on the smooth blade. Did everyone here carry a knife? Pound for pound, this place was more dangerous than a New York City alley after midnight.

"We don't want any trouble." Jackson tried to be diplomatic.

"It's awfully dark tonight, ain't it, Tommy?" The taller one flashed a wicked smile as he turned his attention to Jackson.

"Too dark, Troy," said Tommy. The smile on his face was pure evil.

It took me longer to realize what they were getting at than it did Jackson. His expression was a mixture of defeat and anger.

"Not until you let him go." I should have turned around and left Lenny's fate in the hands of the Rattners, but that would have been wrong. Even I had *some* scruples.

They appeared entertained by my demand and chuckled heartily between them as if I'd told a joke, but this was no laughing matter.

"Tell you what." Troy grinned. "We'll let Porky go, if..."

"If what?" I tried to hold back my irritation, but some of it still came through.

"See that mountain up there?" Tommy pointed over his shoulder.

I followed his hand. It was Finch's place, still hidden in the fog.

"I see it."

"You go up there, and we'll let him go." The sound of his voice, like thick molasses, made me want to stomp the ignorance right out of him. That had been happening a lot lately.

"Anything else?"

"Anything else?" Tommy laughed. "He don't know, does he, brother?"

"What?"

"The Watcher lives up there," said Troy. "He murdered some kids a few years ago, tortured 'em for a week, then cut their hearts out and buried 'em up on the mountain. Maybe he's in a generous mood tonight and he'll kill you quick."

I pretended to be scared.

"He keeps a shotgun up there," said Tommy. "Bring it to us, and we'll consider it payment for your friend."

"And if I don't?"

Troy smiled that wicked smile again. "Then we're all gonna find out what Porky had for dinner, if you know what I mean?"

His brother slid the side of the knife blade along Lenny's stomach.

I knew exactly what he meant. The Rattners might have been dumb as bricks, but they appeared more than capable when it came to violence. They had that thing you needed to be a serial killer. As crazy as it sounded, I knew Lenny Sanders was as good as dead if I didn't get that shotgun for them. I wasn't prepared to have his blood on my hands. Not like that.

I flashed my eyes to Lenny. He could hardly keep his head up, but he could see me, and he shook his head.

"Troy, you go with him," Tommy said. He was the stronger of the two. "We can't have him running to the police." Perhaps they weren't as dumb as I thought.

I left Jackson and Gabe with Tommy. Lenny wasn't going anywhere. It was apparent that Tommy Rattner was mean enough and willing to take all three of them out with a few swings of that knife, especially now that Lenny was disabled. The gravity of the situation was only sinking in as I pressed off into the darkness.

Troy stayed close, keeping his flashlight on me until we reached the foot of the mountain. The fog was all around us now, and I couldn't believe how cold it suddenly felt. I was trying to take my time while I thought of a plan. Though I had been to the old man's house once, I still didn't know what he was capable of, and besides, even if he did like me, I'm sure that wasn't an invitation to rob him. For all I knew, the chances of me winding up dead were about as good as Lenny's at this point.

"There." Troy pointed to the head of a narrow trail with his light. I kept my eyes on it as my feet found the path. It was muddy and slick, so I negotiated the steep ascent as best I could, climbing over the rocks and roots. The higher I climbed, the colder it got. A chill cut right through me.

"Move." There was a tremor in Troy's voice.

I lumbered up the steep incline until we reached the edge of the clearing. The fog was so thick I could barely see my hand in front of my face.

"Get your ass in there and get it," Troy said as we came to a stop.

I could see he was shivering from the cold.

I did as he instructed and crept up the walk, slipped through the iron gate, and approached the porch. The lights were out, which was odd, so I approached the window and peered inside. A lamp was on in the living room. Otherwise, it was dark. I could see the chessboard on the small table; it was exactly as we had left it. I searched the living room and the kitchen, but they were empty, and then caught sight of the gun, propped up against the grandfather clock, exactly where I remembered seeing it.

I glanced back at Troy. He was growing more impatient by the second. He urged me on. I knew the door was unlocked, so I twisted the knob slowly, careful not to make a sound, then pushed it open an inch, then two. When there was enough space for me to slide inside, I did so and found myself in the kitchen. It smelled like bacon. I could see the pan on the stove, the bottom coated in a layer of congealed fat. It had been sitting there a while. My coat was wet from the fog, and my shoes were muddy. I was careful to tread lightly so as not to squeak across the floor or leave a footprint. Holding my breath, I crossed the linoleum to the clock where the gun stood, took hold of it gently, and retraced my steps as I backed toward the door.

Once I was outside, I turned and tossed the gun to Troy, who appeared as stunned as I was that I had actually done it. The next thing we knew, the porch light buzzed to life.

"Shit!" Troy turned for the path, gun in hand. He slipped off the hill and fell from sight.

I ran around the corner of the house, hoping Finch hadn't seen me.

"Who's there?" Finch shouted as he stepped out onto the porch. He sounded angry. Instantly, I regretted what I had done, robbing Peter to pay Paul.

I drifted away from the house until I was hidden behind the rows of corn in the garden. Through an opening, I could see his face. He looked mad as hell as he peered out into the darkness. I watched him mutter a few inaudible words, then turn and go back into the house.

I made it off the mountain, wondering if my theft had been worth it. I didn't think about Lenny until I reached the bottom because I was too busy thinking about myself. Did God understand when you had to do something terrible so something worse wouldn't happen? Maybe I would ask Reverend Ridgeway the next time I saw him—if there would be a next time.

When I made it to the spot where I'd left Gabe and Jackson, it was empty. The only thing that remained was the blood-soaked rope still hanging from the tree. *Damn.* I was too late. I yelled as loud as I could for them, and Jackson answered. I hurried off toward his voice and found the three of them—Jackson, Gabe, and Lenny—standing at the end of the lane beneath the streetlight. Lenny looked awful.

"We need to get him to a doctor." Gabe was trying his best to keep Lenny on his feet.

"What about Tommy and Troy?" I looked around to make sure they weren't waiting for us.

"Gone," Jackson said, "and they took the gun with them."

"How far is the doctor from here?" I asked. Lenny was in no shape to walk.

"Other side of town," said Gabe.

"All right. Let's get him up there." I pointed to one of the few houses that still had its lights on. "I'll knock and see if we can use the phone."

We made Lenny as comfortable as we could on the porch swing, getting some cold rags and ice from Mr. and Mrs. Caldwell. They owned the service station in town. Mr. Caldwell called the hospital in Linville and had them send an ambulance. We all stayed with Lenny until it arrived.

I rode with Lenny to the hospital to make sure he was all right and told Gabe and Jackson to call his dad and have him meet us there. I hated Carl Sanders as much as I hated Lenny, but he deserved to know what had happened.

By the time the doctor took some X-rays and stitched Lenny up, his dad was standing in the waiting room. I saw him through the small window at the top of the door. The only thing that kept running through my mind was that I hoped he wasn't thinking of punishing Lenny for this. I'm not sure he could have taken another beating.

I pushed open the door and waved him back.

"What the hell happened, Lenny?" Carl burst into the room.

"He may not feel much like talking," I said, trying to calm him.

"Did you see who did this?" His eyes were dark and cold.

"The Rattners," I said. "Tommy and Troy."

"I'll kill those bastards," he roared, backhanding a silver tray from the table. It clattered to the floor.

"No!" shouted Lenny, straining to find a voice. "That'll just make things worse."

I could see the fear in his eyes.

Carl appeared confused. I had seen guys like him before; whenever something like this happened, the first thing that came to their mind was revenge. But like Lenny said, it would only have made things worse.

"I think I'm going to leave the two of you to talk." My usefulness had run its course.

I went out into the lobby and used the phone at the nurse's station to call Mom and explained quickly what had happened. I left out the part about stealing the old man's shotgun, of course, but it was still on my conscience and I felt compelled, perhaps for the first time in my life, to get down on my knees and ask God for forgiveness. After a night like this, I needed all the help I could get.

CHAPTER
TEN

*A*TONEMENT

Amanda called me over the following afternoon. It had been over a week since she'd spoken to me, but maybe she had forgiven me for what I had done to Lenny or for breaking my promise or both. Anyway, I didn't care. She had been less than honest with me about the festival, and I had taken my anger out on Lenny. The way I saw it, we were even.

"I heard what you did for Lenny last night," she said as we sat silently on her porch swing. "Few people around here would have helped him."

"Yeah, well, I suppose we all have our moments, don't we?" I wasn't trying to be arrogant, not on purpose anyway, but it was my default, especially when I was wounded. I was still upset with her, though I had moved on from the theory that she had shown up with Rusty out of spite. Unlike me, I don't think she knew how to be malicious. I could feel her staring at me, to the point I became uncomfortable. I refused her the satisfaction of looking into her eyes.

"I'm sorry about the way I acted after the festival," she whispered.

"Sorry? What do you have to be sorry for?"

"I jumped to conclusions without hearing your side of the story. It's just..." Her voice trailed off. "When I saw you that night, sitting on top of Lenny, punching him, I didn't recognize that person." She seemed tormented. "You looked so angry."

"I'm sorry about that." I glanced in her direction. "Lenny's had it coming for a long time, but I never should have acted that way in front of all those people... in front of you." I raised my eyes to her. The dying light of the sun lit her hair, making it appears as if it were on fire. It was only now I noticed the hint of red in it. My heart yearned, and I turned away. I couldn't let myself fall the way I had before, so completely, so foolishly. If I had to withstand another attack like the one I'd suffered at the festival, there would be no need to call an ambulance because I couldn't be saved. "I felt bad as soon as it was over," I admitted after a long pause. "I never wanted to fight Lenny, but he didn't give me much choice. I'm just glad it's all behind us now."

"So am I." She paused and looked away.

"There's something I want to ask you, but don't know how." I tried to twist the words in my head into something marginally acceptable.

"I find the best way to ask a tough question is simply to ask it," she said. It was amusing how she thought of things in the simplest terms. I wondered if it was for my benefit. "Besides, what's the worst that could happen?"

That was an interesting question. The way I saw it, the worst-case scenario involved her slapping me across the face, stomping up to her room, and never speaking to me again. If it tried hard enough, I could already feel the sting on my cheek. On the other hand, the best I could hope for was an explanation of why she was dating Rusty Givens. Either way, I couldn't imagine either outcome leaning in my favor.

"All right." I cleared my throat and worked up as much courage as I had in me. "What's the story with you and Rusty?"

Surely we knew each other well enough where I could ask a question like that. I supposed there was no sense in worrying about it now because the cat was out of the bag, and I felt relieved to have that off my chest. But it was only temporary. I composed myself, drew in a long breath, and braced for the worst.

Amanda stared off into the distance with narrowed eyes. It was always difficult to tell what she was thinking.

"Me and Rusty are... complicated," she said. She flashed her eyes to me, probably to gauge my reaction, then looked away again. "When Mama and I first moved here, I was in sixth grade," she said. "Rusty was a year ahead of me. His family lived up here on the Bluff back then in the house beside yours. That's when I met him for the first time."

This was getting worse by the second. If this story ended with her telling me his dog died, I was going to run to throw myself off the overlook.

"We used to ride bikes and hang out," she continued. "He was the only friend I had other than Kimberly. When his dad got laid off, his parents sold their house and moved down on Llewelyn Street near the grocery store. We kept in touch, but not like before, and after he started high school we sort of drifted apart."

"So what happened?"

"When I started high school, we had geometry class, and I guess we sort of reconnected. We hung out a few times, but that was it, and then this past summer, just before you arrived, he asked me out for ice cream. Mama wasn't thrilled, but I agreed. Over the summer, we went out a few more times and I guess we started dating, though we never made it official."

At least Cindy wasn't totally worthless. I saw no need to continue down this path. It was apparent they had a history, and she had *some* feelings for him, though their depth wasn't clear.

"But it's never going to go anywhere." She changed course unexpectedly.

Finally, perhaps an end to this emotional roller coaster. "Oh?" I tried desperately to conceal my elation.

"He graduates this year, and he'll be off to college. I'll still be here, in Evergreen." She dropped her gaze. By the disappointment in her voice, I knew there was hope for Amanda Davenport, not because she was going to miss Rusty Givens— I couldn't care less about that—but because she, like the supernovas I once studied in science class, was too bright to dim. Someday, she *would* leave Evergreen and be everything she was destined to be. But the one thing I knew about supernovas was that they were unstable, burned hot, and if you were close enough when they imploded, the light show, while impressive, had deadly consequences.

That night I slept better than I had in weeks. I had never been in love before, but surely it had to feel something like this. My insides were constantly in turmoil, and I wanted to be around her all the time even if that meant making excuses so I could do so. I wanted to kiss her, of course, but it was more than that. She made me a better person, and when I was around her, all the anger I had inside seemed to melt away. It was as if a part of me that had been missing all my life was suddenly there.

The next morning, I woke with a purpose; to do whatever it took to win the heart of Amanda Davenport. But first, I had to pay Mr. Finch a visit and explain what had happened with his shotgun. I wasn't entirely sure how he would take the news that I had robbed him, but I could no longer take the guilt that was eating away at me.

After breakfast, I set out for the mountain. Now that I had been there twice, I was able to avoid the places where it was easy to slip and fall. A week ago, if someone had told me I would be on the mountain twice and headed back for the third time, I would have thought they were crazy. Yet here I was.

When I got to the clearing, I saw first the light on the porch, then the front door standing slightly ajar. I pushed through the open gate and went up to the porch and called for him.

"That you, Cole?" he asked.

"Yes sir, Mr. Finch. It's me. Is it all right if I come in? There's something I need to talk to you about."

He welcomed me inside and was already at the table in the living room, staring down at the pieces on the board.

"You come to continue our game?" he asked hopefully.

"Yes sir." I hesitated. "But I have something I need to tell you first."

His cold, dark eyes rose from the board as I rounded the sofa.

My hands were clammy, and there was a lump in my throat as I sat down. Something about his face was different today, younger if that was possible. Also the scowl, which was pronounced the last time I was here, had loosened. It made what I had to say that much harder. I questioned my decision to tell him the truth. Surely it would have been easier to lie. Too late. I was already there, three feet away from him. I considered my escape route if things went poorly.

"About last night," I began, finding a voice. It sounded foreign to me, as if I was having one of those out-of-body experiences.

"Yes?" he said quietly, his eyes still on me.

"I'm the one who took your shotgun. But I had to," I said quickly, "or someone was going to die." I held my breath as I waited for the worst.

"I know," he said plainly, dropping his gaze back to the board as he centered his pawns. "I figured you had a good reason, or you wouldn'a done it. Rules change when someone's life hangs in the balance."

The way he said it made me think he had experience in this area. I wasn't sure what to say. Was this what I had been dreading? I knew then that Gabe and Jackson were wrong about Old Man Finch. He wasn't a murderer, at least not in the sense that everyone thought he was. I presumed he had killed before in war, but that was different. No man could have served as long as he had without taking a life. But there was a difference between killing in war and in civilian life. My dad had mentioned it once. I was sure he had killed before as well, though we never asked him about it.

"I will get it back for you," I promised, now studying the pieces as I pondered my next move.

"I know you will." He raised his eyes to mine. There it was again, that flash of evil. It didn't frighten me but let me know he was still dangerous when he needed to be.

We traded several moves before the game bogged down. The first few moves are always simple; there's little risk in them, but they set the tone for the game. So once you're a dozen moves in, you think about offense versus defense and potential pitfalls. Chess was a thinking-man's game, and maybe that's the reason I liked it so much, because it made me concentrate. After all, chess was like life—slow, steady, calculated, but one wrong move, one miscalculation, and you were destined for defeat. There is nothing more crushing than the prolonged agony of watching your most powerful pieces be eliminated one by one.

At half past twelve, Mr. Finch got up from the table and stretched his legs. He went into the kitchen to make lunch and asked if I would like to stay. I told him I had to be going because I had promised my mother I would clean my room but that I would return later in the week and continue our game. At this rate, it would take until Christmas to determine a winner, but maybe that's what he intended. I took Finch for a lonely man, isolated from the rest of the world. He was marooned on that mountain, an island in a sea of pines.

By the time I made it home, Mom and Tabitha had already eaten and were sitting in the living room watching cartoons. That was their Saturday afternoon routine. It had once been my routine as well but not in a very long time. I grabbed a sandwich from the kitchen and went to my room to think. But before I sat down, I looked out the window at Amanda's place to see if she was home. Sometimes I would see her sitting on the porch swing. She'd rock for hours, most times with a book in her hand. She read more than anyone I had ever met, and I often wondered if she did it to escape the monotony of Evergreen.

I should have been reading myself. Mrs. Courtney was giving us a test on *Animal Farm* in a few days, and I was still stuck in chapter two, but the truth is I wasn't much for books unless it had something to do with math or science. A story about pigs taking over a farm as a metaphor for the Russian Revolution didn't exactly leave me yearning for more. I bet Amanda had already read it, probably in an afternoon spent among the trees. Sometimes I wondered what it would be like to see the world through her eyes.

After an hour of staring mindlessly at the TV, I got on my bike and rode to the Flats. My hope of getting a car had all but faded, especially after Mom had discovered I had been in a fight. She said if I wasn't mature enough to control my temper, then driving was out of the question. It wasn't as if everyone in town had a car anyway except the adults who had to drive to Linville to work. Most everyone else walked or rode bikes, so at least I didn't feel entirely out of place.

It was short enough to walk, but the bike was more convenient and would be faster if I needed to make a quick exit. I wasn't especially thrilled about passing the abandoned houses on James Street, but I needed to make sure Lenny had made it home from the hospital. Sometimes I wondered why I even cared, but if I thought about it long enough, I knew deep down Lenny was a guy who was damaged. After Dad died, I wanted to be mean, even *was* to some people, but it didn't suit me. I always wound up feeling sorry after I had said or done something I shouldn't have. I suppose it came easy for people like the Rattners or Ricky and Derek, but not me. I was cursed with a kind heart.

All the lights were off at Amanda's house as I rode by. She was probably shopping with her mother. I wondered what that must be like, trudging around town all day with Cindy Davenport, going from store to store, stopping along the way to trade scintillating tidbits of gossip. Amanda must have been there to hold the bags, nod, smile at her mother's jokes, and reaffirm her faith in church camp. It sounded like the most miserable existence I could imagine.

I made it to James Street and passed the row of haunted houses, which were not as imposing as the first time I'd seen them. Looking through the windows that weren't boarded up, I was astonished to find stone fireplaces and crown molding. They needed a lot of work, but perhaps in my haste to cast them aside, I had failed to recognize the beauty within.

The one place I hadn't misjudged was Lenny's house. I pulled off the side of the road after crossing the little bridge and laid my bike down on the edge of the yard. This time when I made it to the door, I didn't hesitate and rapped loudly on the front door. When Carl Sanders opened it, I asked to see Lenny, and he went and fetched him immediately. He also didn't appear as imposing as before. I suppose when you're nervous, your mind can play tricks on you.

Lenny lumbered to the door and stepped out onto the porch. His arm was in a sling, and his face was black and blue, but at least there was no blood. He looked like he'd been run over by a truck.

"Hey, Cole," he said glumly.

"How are you feeling?" I asked, but he didn't need to answer. I already knew just by looking at him.

"It looks worse than it is," he said. "The arm's broken and Doc Coffee said I'll have to get a cast next week, but other than that, I'll survive."

We stood there for a couple of minutes, neither one of us knowing what to say. Then, out of the blue, I got the shock of my life.

"I guess I should thank you for saving my life," he said, looking down. "And I wanted to say I'm sorry."

"You're welcome... and thanks." I knew how hard this must be for him.

"I told my dad what happened at the festival. He was plenty mad at me."

"He didn't..." My voice trailed off. I wanted to ask if he had beaten him again, but I hoped he wouldn't, especially given his condition. "So does this mean we're..." I couldn't bring myself to say *friends*. That would have been more than my mind could handle.

"We're cool," he said. "Truce?" He spit in his left hand, the one that wasn't broken.

I stared at it for a minute. This gesture wasn't familiar to me, so I did as he did and spit in my hand. "Truce," I said, sealing our cease-fire with a handshake. What a relief. I never had to worry about Lenny Sanders again. Now I just had to make sure word made its way to Derek and Ricky.

"I need your help," said Lenny after a pause.

"With what?"

"I gotta find a way to get back at Tommy and Troy."

I thought about that for a few long seconds before answering. "Maybe we can help each other."

He gave me a strange look.

"I've got to get Old Man Finch's shotgun back from them," I explained. "I promised him I would."

"He knows you took it?"

"I told him this morning," I confessed.

"I swear to God, you must have cast a spell on him." Lenny chuckled.

I did the same. "He's actually not that bad. I think he got a bad rap somehow, and I want to do what I can to clear his name. Gabe and Jackson have been helping me look into the death of those teens from Linville."

"Well, if you need my help, all you have to do is ask."

Before I left, we shook hands again, and I watched as Lenny retreated inside.

When I left his house, I couldn't believe my luck. Just two weeks earlier, I was within a heartbeat of breathing my last breath, and now we were friends—well, nearly. Now if I could only find a way to connect with Amanda.

CHAPTER
ELEVEN

THE FLOOD

My mother was the most predictable person I had ever met. That is until we moved to Evergreen. In eight months, she had gone from wife to widow, full-time sales executive to stay-at-home mom, had taken up and mastered the art of cooking, began painting, and had read more books than I would ever read in a lifetime. It was as though she had hit the reset button. I figured most of it was driven by her determination to make the best of an unpleasant situation. After all, my father's death had hit her especially hard, and without him around, she was forced to be both mother and father, something I found unenviable at best.

By the time November rolled around, I'd all but given up hope of ever getting a car. I'd been in my fair share of trouble over the whole Lenny situation, and although I appeared to have somewhat redeemed myself by what I'd done to save him from Tommy and Troy, Mom still didn't know the whole story, and God willing, she never would. Still, I needed my own car. I would be seventeen in a few months, and everyone knew if you were that old and without a car, surely something must be wrong with you.

Then, on a Friday afternoon, something truly unexpected happened. When I got home from school, I noticed a vehicle sitting in our driveway. It was a new Ford Mustang, red with a black stripe down the center. I had wanted one for as long as I could remember. What were the odds? I crept my way toward the front door.

"Mom?" I stepped into the foyer, still admiring the beautiful machine that sat in the driveway.

"Hey, Cole." She emerged from the kitchen, drying her hands with a towel.

"Whose car is that?"

She tossed a set of keys to me and smiled, then disappeared back into the kitchen as if nothing had happened.

But something had happened—something extraordinary. A jolt of electricity went straight through me.

"You're welcome." She poked her head around the corner.

I had to pinch myself to make sure I wasn't dreaming.

"Holy sh—"

"Cole!"

"Sorry. I mean thank you." I looked down at the keys again, feeling the weight of them in my hands. "Holy shit," I whispered to myself.

"New car," said Tabitha, holding on to Mom's leg as they appeared in the hallway.

"Yeah, Tabby, new car. Can I?" I flashed the keys as I looked at my mom.

She nodded and told me to be careful.

Aside from the car, there was only one thing I had on my

mind. I turned the key, and the engine roared to life. It was exhilarating to have that much power at my fingertips. What a rush. I took a minute to familiarize myself with the controls, then I backed out of the drive and pulled up to Amanda's house and honked the horn. She came out a moment later with a puzzled look on her face.

"Is this...?"

"Mine," I said, grinning broadly.

"Whoa!" She bent down and looked inside. "You're so lucky."

"Hop in," I said.

She ran back to the house and told her mother she was going for a drive, then climbed in and we sped off. I had the windows down and the radio up the entire way.

"This is amazing. When did you get it?"

"Just now. It was waiting in the driveway for me when I got home."

"I love this car," she said, admiring the interior as the wind blew through her hair. My eyes were on the road, but I could feel her staring at me for a long time. Between the exhilaration of the car and her sitting beside me, I could hardly keep it between the yellow lines.

That afternoon we drove all around the Piedmont—from Evergreen all the way over to Asheville and back—stopping at McDonald's for a burger on the way home. I had never seen Amanda smile as much as she did that day.

"Have you ever thought about what you want to do when you leave Evergreen?" I asked as we entered the town limits. I glanced at the clock on the radio—six fifteen. What remained of the sun was behind us, slowly fading into a blood-red sky.

"Leave Evergreen?" she asked as if it was the furthest thing from her mind.

"After high school. Surely, you don't want to hang around here, do you?" I figured if anyone made a break when they were eighteen, it would be here. She had so many things going for her.

She appeared perplexed by my question.

She hesitated. "I don't know. I was thinking of going to college somewhere close by, maybe Appalachian State or Mars Hill, so I can be near Mama."

"Don't you want to get away from here?"

"Where would I go?" She looked down and turned away.

"I don't know, some place crazy like New York or LA" I glanced in her direction. She was still peering out into the darkness.

"I don't know about that," she said nervously. "What if I'm not cut out for places like that? I've never been anywhere bigger than Atlanta."

"Don't sell yourself short, Amanda." I enjoyed saying her name aloud. It sounded natural in my head, as if we were destined to be together. While I waited for her to respond, I said it once more to myself.

"You're always so sure," she said, turning her gaze upon me.

"About you, yes." I looked at her, then back to the road.

"I like days like this," she said happily.

"So do I."

When we pulled onto Old Lockwood Road, the day ended much the same way it began, with my hopes as high as they'd been since we moved to Evergreen. I stopped the car in front of her house, and she hesitated before getting out.

"I want you to know something," she whispered. "No one else knows this, but about a month before you and your family moved to Evergreen, I had a dream about you."

"Me? But that's impossible."

"Mama says they're premonitions. I have dreams some-times... see things before they happen. I thought little of it until I had the same dream again a few days later. When I met you on the porch that day, I knew it was you I had seen."

A chill ran through me.

"What do you think it means?"

"Something—fate, destiny, whatever you want to call it—brought us together." She turned away. "Anyway, I just thought you should know."

What do you say to someone who tells you they dreamed about you before you even met? I was at a loss for words. Once I had recovered, I thanked her for spending the afternoon with me and told her I would see her tomorrow.

That night, Amanda Davenport appeared in my dreams for the first time. Given all the time we'd spent together, I was surprised she had not dominated my dreams long before now, but I suppose you can't think about the same thing all the time. Still, it was frustrating because no matter how hard I tried, it felt like there was a barrier between us I could not overcome. I'd had every opportunity to kiss her that night, but I didn't, and I hated myself for it.

As Amanda had predicted, I received an invitation to Kimberly's party. It was on Saturday at four o'clock at the convention center. By my standards, it was an ordinary banquet hall and couldn't have seated more than a hundred people. Still, it was the nicest place in Evergreen and was reserved for weddings and parties, though only the wealthiest of Evergreen's residents could afford it.

When it came to his only daughter, Robert Davis spared no expense. As Amanda told me, Kimberly was the first one in our class to have a car when she turned sixteen, a new BMW, which in Evergreen might as well have been a Lamborghini.

After the night at the festival, it was apparent that Kimberly had something of a crush on me, but I tried to stay focused on Amanda.

———

THEY HAD DECORATED the convention center to look like the beach, sand and all. Kimberly and her family vacationed on Hilton Head Island two weeks out of every summer, so she wanted to re-create that in Evergreen.

Amanda was already there when I arrived, helping Kimberly put the finishing touches on the tablescapes. I added my gift to the mountain of others on display inside the door and found a seat beside Sean Yancey, a guy from my history class. He already looked bored.

"Some party, huh?" I tried to make small talk.

"Do you believe this shit?" he asked. "Sand... water... seashells? She thinks she's hot shit because of her dad."

I played along, but only for a minute. This was the one event I thought would be free of drama, but any notion of that quickly faded.

"Hey, Cole." Kimberly appeared as if from nowhere. She leaned in and gave me a hug.

"Hey, Kimberly," I said, patting her cordially on the back. I could see Amanda standing at the table from the other side of the room. I gave a look of bewilderment. She smiled.

By the time the party started, there were sixty-five guys and girls there, almost all of whom I recognized. It was awkward at first, but it didn't take long before everyone moved to the dance floor once the music started. Everyone but me. I wasn't much of a dancer, and by that, I mean I wasn't a dancer at all. There had been an incident at a middle school dance that I was sure I would never live down.

"So are you having a good time?" Amanda found me alone at one of the tables.

"Sure," I said, trying to disguise my sarcasm. "You?"

"I am, but my feet are killing me."

"Have a seat." I pulled the chair out for her.

She smiled. "Thanks. I enjoyed the road trip yesterday."

"Me too. I'm glad you could go. Maybe we can go again sometime?"

"I'd like that."

I was working up the courage to ask her something personal, something I had wanted to ask for weeks, but as I was set to deliver my question, Kimberly showed up and dragged Amanda out onto the dance floor. It seemed no matter how many times I tried to talk to her, something always got in the way. Sometimes I thought fate was working against us.

After the party, Amanda stayed to help clean up, and I went home. A storm was brewing—a big storm—so I put away the last Halloween decorations and discarded the pumpkins in the trash. If the storm was as bad as they had predicted, the last thing I wanted was to be chasing pumpkins and tombstones all over the neighborhood.

That night, as the remnants of Hurricane Juan spread north out of the Gulf of Mexico, it brought with it a series of storms the likes of which Evergreen had not seen in over half a century. The rain and wind lashed out at the town as if it were being punished by God himself. Lightning split the sky, and thunder rolled in echoing waves across the valley. The rains lasted for seven days and seven nights. It was biblical.

I woke in the middle of the night to the sound of rain hammering on the roof above me. Unable to sleep, I sat up and stared out the window toward the mountain; it was shrouded in darkness. I wondered how Finch was faring in the storm. Lightning always struck the highest places first, and his house was on one of the highest ridges surrounding Evergreen.

As I lay back down and tried to sleep, my thoughts drifted to the Rattner twins. I pictured them laughing about how they had tricked me into stealing Finch's gun. More disturbing than that was what would have happened had we not shown up when we did. I shuddered to think of what they would have done to poor Lenny.

Weeks passed, and as the trees shed what remained of their leaves and Thanksgiving approached, things settled. No one had seen Tommy or Troy since Halloween, and we all assumed they were lying low. There was the outside chance Carl Sanders had tracked them down and killed them, but it wasn't likely. There was also the possibility that they had been swept up in the flood. Either way, I didn't care. They were gone, and that was all that mattered.

It took weeks to clean up the devastation left in the wake

of the rains. The lowest areas of town, starting at the river and working back along Hanley Creek, had been under several feet of water for more than a week, which meant everything from the fairgrounds to the center of town was a mess of mud and debris. Most folks said it was the worst flood they had seen since the deluge of '45 when the water made it all the way to the bank's steps.

It was difficult to appreciate the true magnitude of the event unless you could see it from above. My spot on the Bluff provided such a view. From my front porch, I had seen the water rise slowly at first, then more rapidly as the days of rain took their toll. The river had jumped the banks and inched its way toward town, swallowing it block by block. When it was all over, the southern half of the town was submerged beneath a shallow lake. The sight was incomprehensible.

They canceled school all week, and on Friday morning after breakfast, I threw on some old jeans and a coat and went to the garage to get my bike. With the streets a mess, I didn't want to risk scuffing up my new car. Now that I was a resident of Evergreen, I figured that the sensible and responsible thing to do was go into town and see if I could help. The guys agreed to meet at Milford's.

I had to take an alternate route because James Street was still impassable, so I turned north toward the school and took the long way. When I was a couple of blocks from Milford's, I skidded my bike to a stop at the line of demarcation. On one side of the mud line, everything was as it had been before the rains started—wet but intact. On the other side, everything was encased in a layer of silt. Homes were ruined, contents scattered across yards, in the streets, and in many places, clothes and curtains hung from the trees like Spanish moss.

I saw no way to get to Milford's, and if the water had reached all the way up to Shannon Street, there was no way it wouldn't be knee-deep at the Alley. I wondered if the fort had survived.

"Cole." I turned to find Charlie and Jackson speeding down the hill.

"You guys believe this shit?" I indicated the devastation in front of me.

"Yeah, it's crazy," said Charlie.

"I don't think we can get to Milford's." Jackson said what Charlie and I were already thinking.

"Where do we even start?" I looked at the giant mess before us. It was going to take an entire army to get this place cleaned up.

"Fellas." We turned our heads to find Chief Morris creeping up Kendall Avenue in his patrol car. He came to a stop in front of us. "What are you boys doing down here? You should be home where it's safe."

"We came to help," announced Charlie.

"That's neighborly, but I'm afraid there isn't much we can do until the Guard gets here." I had an uncle who at one time served in the National Guard. They were called in to help with natural disasters, but from what I had heard on the news, there were other places along the Gulf Coast and into the south that were in far worse shape than Evergreen, though as I turned an eye back to the ravaged houses, it found that difficult to imagine.

"There has to be something we can do," said Jackson.

Chief Morris thought for a moment. "Well, if you're up to it, they could use some help down at Milford's getting all the tools cleaned up and back on the shelves. I'm sure Don would appreciate you guys lending a hand."

We all agreed to do it.

"Do you know a way to get there?" I asked, seeing the state of the road in front of us.

"You can take Shannon all the way into town, then hang a left on Corwyn. It's tough going though, so you may have to get there on foot."

We ditched our bikes at the corner of Shannon and Kendall and trudged through the mud until we got to Milford's. Typically it was only a ten-minute walk, but it took us the better part of an hour to wade through the slop. Thank God it wasn't summer, or the copperheads and rattlesnakes would have been all over the place.

When we arrived, we could see Don Milford out in the parking lot, pushing the mud with a snowplow that he'd fitted to the front of his pickup. Nothing like Southern ingenuity.

"Mr. Milford," called Charlie, getting his attention.

"You guys here to help?" asked Don.

"Yes sir," we all said.

He put the truck in idle and showed us inside. Everything was encased in a thick layer of silt that felt like fine-grain sand. It would take a month and a miracle to get this place back to normal.

Jackson, Charlie, and I went about washing all the tools, drying them, and placing them back on the shelves. Eric and Scott joined us an hour later. They had come in from the other side of town, where they said it was far worse. My heart went out to the folks in the Flats. Gabe showed up a half hour after the Shoffners. He was bent over and out of breath.

"This is some crazy shit." Gabe grabbed a towel and wiped the mud from his face.

"I've never seen anything like this," I admitted, over-whelmed by it all. Then I realized—had anyone heard from Lenny? From my house, I could see his, and it had surprised me it was still standing. "Any of you guys hear from Lenny?" I asked. Silence.

"Not that it's any of my business," said Eric, "but I didn't think you'd care."

I forgot that none of them knew about the deal he and I made. I explained what had happened the week before, though I could tell none of them believed me.

Lenny Sanders' ears must have been burning because the next time the front door to Milford's opened, he walked in, looking angry as ever.

"Cole." He staggered toward us like a creature from one of my comics.

"Lenny," I replied cautiously.

He was within a foot of me, glaring at the others as they waited intently to see what would happen next. I'm sure they thought he was going to hit me, but he didn't. Instead, he stuck out his hand. It reminded me of the story of Noah and sending the dove as the peace offering. I supposed Lenny was the dove in this metaphor, though that was a stretch. Anyway, I shook his hand, and he agreed to help. The looks on the faces of my friends were priceless.

Long about dark, when we left Milford's, me, Charlie, and Jackson went back to Shannon Street and jumped on our bikes while Lenny, Gabe, and the Shoffners set off in the other direc-tion. I wasn't sure I had the strength to get home.

We all agreed to meet back up tomorrow. The road to healing was a long one, but we would do our part to help.

———

AFTER ANOTHER WEEK of no school, we were back in class on the Monday before the holiday. Thanksgiving was only a few days off, but it would take on a different meaning this year. Instead of being thankful for material possessions, I was grateful for my family and friends because no one had lost their lives in the storms. It was difficult for me to wrap my head around just how lucky we all were.

I figured after everything that had happened, another trip to church couldn't hurt. I had a guilty conscience over taking Finch's shotgun and would not feel better until it was where it belonged, back up on the mountain. This time, I didn't go with Amanda. Instead, I asked my mom and sister if they would like to go. Mom seemed shocked that I had asked her but was delighted. I think I even saw a tear in her eye, which she blamed on her allergies. She gave me a speech about how she felt I was growing up. Thank God she finally noticed.

Mom even let me drive them to church in my car, which was a surprise. As we ascended through the cut in the trees, listening to the radio, I couldn't help but think Cindy's plan had worked after all. Here we were—me, Tabitha, and Mom—pulling up to the White Hall Baptist Church. If you'd told me that three months ago, I would have said you were crazy, probably fought you, but here we were just the same, all dressed in our Sunday best, ready for our weekly dose of Jesus.

Amanda might have been the most surprised that we were all

there. Her eyes were as wide as saucers as she turned around and saw us take up a seat on the right side, a few rows in front of Lenny and Carl. I turned to her and smiled. Honestly, I would have rather sat with her, but I couldn't abandon Mom and Tabitha.

Reverend Ridgeway was filled with the spirit that morning, and he was more animated than the first time I had seen him, if that were possible. He preached a sermon on Thanksgiving, which I figured was appropriate given it was just around the corner.

"Rejoice evermore," he boomed. "Pray without ceasing. In everything give thanks, for this is the will of God in Christ Jesus concerning you."

I struggled to think about giving thanks for all things because the way I saw it, not all things were not worthy of thanks. Was I supposed to give thanks for Tommy and Troy Rattner beating Lenny within an inch of his life? Or what about me stealing the gun for them? The longer I thought about it, the more bewildered I became.

"But do not lose faith," he said as if sensing my dismay. "For God hears your heart, sees your troubles, and never forsakes you."

Believe it or not, I felt marginally better.

THAT AFTERNOON I found myself on the front porch reading what remained of *Animal Farm*. There was a test on it in two days, and with all I had been doing to help the town, I was way behind with my schoolwork. Surely my quest to help the residents of Evergreen was nobler than algebra and novel reading. At least it justified my procrastination. I was halfway through chapter nine, trying to stay focused as the animals rebuilt the windmill, when I got the sense someone was watching me.

"Hey, Cole." Amanda waved as she glided up the walk.

She was wearing an orange dress with a denim jacket and boots that stopped just below her knees. Her hair was longer now, a few inches below her shoulders, but despite the cooler weather, she kept her tan. I was amazed at how her blue eyes sparkled against the denim.

"Hey." I marked my place in the book and set it to the side. "Do you want to sit?"

"You still not finished with that?" She chuckled as she tucked her dress beneath her and sat with her legs crossed on the swing.

"Yeah, well, I like to take my time," I said. "Besides, it's not exactly my kind of story."

"Mine either."

"So what's going on?" She seemed more cheerful than usual.

"I have to tell you, when I saw you guys in church this morning, I couldn't believe my eyes." She was smiling now.

"I would have sat with you, but..."

"Oh, that's all right. Besides, I'm sure your mom appreciated you staying with her. I don't think she took the smile off her face the whole time you were there."

"I guess you're right." I hadn't noticed. "So what did you come over for?"

"Why? You don't want me to be here?" she said half-jokingly.

"No—it's not that." I caught myself. "It's just I didn't know if there was a particular reason or not."

"No. I just thought we hadn't talked in a while and wanted to see what you were up to."

"Yeah, about that," I said. "I haven't been ignoring you or anything, it's just Don put us to work cleaning up the store after the flood. It took two weeks to get the place back in order, but I think it looks better than before."

"Us?"

I looked skyward as I tried to remember. "Me, Gabe, and Jackson of course." I counted with my fingers. "Then there was Charlie, the Shoffners, and Lenny."

"I didn't think I'd ever see the day when you and Lenny could be in the same room at the same time without wanting to kill each other. I'm glad though. It makes me think there's still hope in the world."

She was always thinking big picture, and sometimes I got lost trying to keep up with her, but I didn't care. I loved the chase.

"Listen," she said. "I was talking with Kimberly the other day, and there's something she wanted me to ask you."

"Okay..." Why was it every time she asked me a question, I got the strange feeling something terrible was coming?

"What do you think about her?"

"She's cool," I said, not fully understanding where this line of questioning was headed. "Why do you ask?"

"Well, there's a dance coming up in a couple of weeks—the Blizzard Ball. I'm sure you've heard them mention it at school. And well, we—I mean she was wondering if you'd want to go."

My head was turning in circles. I had a tendency to get things jumbled up whenever a question took me by surprise. Was Amanda asking me for herself or for Kimberly? I was confident I knew the answer, but I had to be sure. "With Kimberly?"

"Yeah. I think the two of you would make a great couple."

She should have been a surgeon as many times as she had ripped my heart out. I clenched my jaw tightly, trying to keep the anger from twisting my face into a Dr. Jekyll/Mr. Hyde situation, but it took every ounce of strength I had.

"I'll have to think about it," I said through gritted teeth, forcing myself not to sound harsh.

"Oh." She looked surprised, but what did she expect? "Well, okay. I won't say anything to Kimberly then."

We sat there in awkward silence for a few more minutes. I stared straight ahead as my mind raced. I was as mad as I had been that night at the festival, but I fought hard to keep it from showing.

Amanda left soon after, but I remained on the porch swing for a long time that evening. I was too angry to read, so I just sat there staring off toward the end of the cul-de-sac at Mr. Sampson, who was trimming the maple in his front yard.

CHAPTER

TWELVE

FRIDAY, DECEMBER 13, 1985

They say nothing good happens on Friday the Thirteenth, and I'm living proof of that. When I was nine, I broke my arm during a hockey game. The following year, I had my tooth knocked out in a fight, and when I was fourteen, I fell on my way to my home from school and dislocated my knee. Given my track record, when I found out the Blizzard Ball fell on the thirteenth, I had little hope that it would be anything but another disaster.

Ever since being talked into taking Kimberly weeks earlier, I had been dreading the dance. Amanda was delighted, but I think it was mostly because she didn't need to worry about me asking her as long as I had someone to go with. I resented her for manipulating me the way she had, but I was equally upset with myself for allowing it to happen.

Jackson took Jennifer Dalman, a cheerleader and someone who had been after him for months, and Gabe went with

Marie Helton, the homecoming queen, though Jackson and I both believed she was a little out of his league. We still weren't sure how he pulled that off.

We all met up at the diner before the dance. For my sake and, perhaps more importantly, hers, I was hoping Amanda and Rusty stayed away.

"Do you want something to drink?" I asked Kimberly.

"Coke please." She batted her brown eyes at me.

Kimberly was a nice girl, pretty too in that girl-next-door, unassuming sort of way, so I felt bad for leading her on, but what choice did I have? This whole charade was Amanda's fault, so if things went sideways—and I fully expected they would at some point—she would be the one to blame.

I returned with two Cokes and slid into the booth opposite Kimberly. The others were in the booth behind us.

"So," she began, sipping her Coke through a red straw, "I'm dying to see what decorations they came up with this year. Last year was red and gold." She had a look of disgust on her face.

"Not your colors?" I pretended to be interested.

"Blue is my color. After that, it doesn't matter. Silver or gold would be nice, but..." Her voice fell off. "How do you feel about slow songs?" she asked apprehensively.

"I, um..." I must have looked like I was trying to solve the most difficult math problem in the world. I had never danced with a girl in my life, let alone to a slow song, though I imagined it had to be infinitely easier than a fast one. After all, how difficult could it be to sway back and forth for a couple of minutes? Suddenly, I felt strangely uncomfortable. "They're okay." I forced a smile.

I should have contemplated the possibilities of this dance,

but I had been so mad about the whole thing, I wasn't thinking clearly. I was a lot of things, but a dancer wasn't one of them. I blamed it on my two left feet. Mom said my dad was the same way. I saw a film with them dancing at their wedding. It looked more like a controlled seizure than dancing.

"You don't have to if you don't want." She looked away.

"No, I don't mind. It's just I'm not that great at dancing, so..."

"Oh, that's all right." She sounded relieved. "Neither am I. Two left feet." She pointed down at her sparkling blue shoes.

We both got a laugh out of that.

When we arrived at school, our friends were already there. Admittedly, Kimberly and I made a good couple, at least from a distance, but I would have much rather been there with Amanda. Nevertheless, I was resigned to enjoying myself, so I tried my best to forget about Amanda as we stepped in front of the camera for our picture. A half hour went by, and I felt more confident I could make the best of this night—that was until *she* walked in.

Life itself stopped whenever Amanda walked into a room. Everyone turned to look at her as if she were an angel and had stepped out of heaven to grace us with her presence. I hated myself for looking, but it was as involuntary as breathing. She wore a long silver dress that looked as if it were made only for her. I stood there in awe of the most beautiful girl I had ever laid eyes on. I was enraptured—and I knew I had stared too long when I felt Kimberly's eyes staring a hole in the side of my head.

"He got dressed up, didn't he?" I said jokingly, grasping at something to say that made me appear less guilty.

162

I glanced at Kimberly.

"What?"

"No tie." I pointed at Rusty, who was wearing a sport coat over a blue-and-green flannel shirt. Did he own anything other than flannel?

She turned and looked. "You're right!" She hid her face in my arm and stifled a laugh, then looked up. "For a second there I thought you were..." Her voice faded, but I knew what she was thinking.

I pasted a look of confusion on my face. "What?"

"Never mind," she said.

After we got some punch, Mrs. Winthrop found us and showed us to our seats. They were assigned of course. I glanced at the other name tags at our table, hoping that Amanda and Rusty had been placed somewhere else. After all, what were the odds? I probably could have produced a relatively decent answer if I had thought about it for a minute, but I was busy scanning the cards.

WHITNEY SLOVER, GARY SINGLETON, CHAD MURPHY, DELILA WILLIAMS... I was gaining confidence with each one that wasn't Amanda. There were only two left. My eyes drifted to the first. To my horror, written in perfect calligraphic script was the one name I couldn't get away from no matter how hard I tried. It was official, fate or the universe, or God himself had it in for me.

"Hey, guys." Her voice cut like a knife, but I turned and forced a smile.

"Hey!" Kimberly shrieked as if this was the greatest night of her life.

Rusty and I shook hands cordially, but that's as far as the pleasantries went. He looked old enough to be a sophomore in college. I didn't envy Rusty for his looks, athletic ability, or intelligence. I had him bested in all categories except the one that counted—gaining Amanda's affection—and wondered if my soul could hold on long enough for him to go to college and hopefully never return.

I had been dreading the dancing part of the Blizzard Ball ever since Kimberly had mentioned it earlier at the diner. Still, now that it began, anything was better than sitting at the table watching Rusty whisper into Amanda's ear. Strength was my strong suit, but even I had my limits.

I got up from the table, took Kimberly's hand, and led her out onto the floor. She had no objections, so we did the best we could. Despite our fear, we blended in with all the others who had absolutely no idea what they were doing, and we did that until the music stopped. We got something to drink and went back to the table. It was empty. Amanda and Rusty were on the other side of the room talking to Rusty's friends from the football team. I was sure the conversation was riveting.

After we waited for the music to return, Kimberly asked if I wanted to try a slow one.

"Why not?" I sighed. This time, she led me slowly out onto the floor.

Somewhere between my being pissed off at Amanda and the joy on Kimberly's face, I felt a shift inside me. Amanda obviously had no intentions of breaking up with Rusty despite my advances, so I figured I might as well make the most of the situation. After all, Kimberly had pursued me, not the other way around, and suddenly I felt bad for putting her through the same agony I was going through with Amanda.

"I was worried about tonight," I admitted, as we kept with the rhythm of the music.

She tilted her head slightly to the side. "Why?"

"I don't know. I never did things like this back home. The girls there were different."

"Their loss." She stared longingly into my eyes.

Suddenly, a wave of heat washed over me, and I felt a little faint. Maybe it was the music or the way Kimberly's eyes sparkled beneath the lights or the perfume she had on, but whatever it was, the space between us narrowed. She was close enough that her cool breath grazed my neck, and it sent my heart racing. I felt the overwhelming need to say something, but my mind was cloudy. Instinct took over, and the next thing I knew, her lips were touching mine. A rush of excitement, the kind you get when you're falling or driving really fast, coursed through my veins. The kiss couldn't have lasted for more than a few seconds, but as I withdrew and opened my eyes, I gazed at her, wondering if it had the same effect on her.

A warm smile broke across her face as she let out a sigh. She rested her head on my chest. As much as I had dreamed about my first kiss being with Amanda, none of that mattered now. Down deep, I hoped she had seen it, but honestly, I didn't care. I was tired of being hurt. We snuck out the back a little after eleven, and I drove Kimberly home. We talked the whole way there. About how unbelievably great we were at dancing—not—about how much fun we had, and about the kiss. I promised to call her the next day, and before she got out of the car, she leaned over and kissed me good night. As I drove home, I kept thinking it was the best night of my life.

When I pulled up outside Amanda's house Monday morning and waited to take her to school, I hoped she had already left. I regretted ever agreeing to take her. Since she still couldn't convince her mom and Ronnie to get her a car, what had seemed like a brilliant plan at the time was now a gigantic pain in my ass.

"Some dance." Lenny slid into the back seat. I was glad he was coming with us today. Hopefully, he could keep my mind off her.

"Yeah, it was. Who'd you go with again?" I remembered seeing him there, but I'd been so wrapped up with Kimberly I hadn't said hello.

"Tiffany Dewitt. She lives over in Linville." I wondered how someone like Lenny could get a girl at all, but despite his looks, he wasn't a complete train wreck as long as you weren't on his bad side.

It was nice to ride to school without looking over my shoulder. Now that Lenny and I were friends, I had nothing to fear except Amanda, and she was far more terrifying because I had no defense against her. As she slid into the passenger seat, the familiar smell of lavender filled the air. I watched her hair sparkling in the sunlight. Damn—why did she have to always look so good?

"Hey, buddy." She slapped me on the shoulder. That's what every guy wants to hear from the girl they're madly in love with.

"Hey," I said indifferently. My eyes were dead ahead as I started toward school.

"Everything all right?" Undoubtedly, she recognized the change in my demeanor. Usually, I was the one trying to keep the conversation lively, trying to pull her along so she would find me irresistible, but those days were over. Now she would get the darker, indifferent side of Cole Mercer.

"Yep. Fine."

"So I talked to Kimberly this weekend." She nudged my ribs with her elbow.

"And?"

"She would not stop talking about the dance. I've been friends with Kimberly for a long time, and I don't think I've ever seen her so excited. You can thank me for that one later." She looked as if she had done me a favor. I could feel the anger swelling inside me.

"Thank you?" I asked, eyes tight.

The tone of my voice took her off guard. She leaned away from me and shot a crooked smile to Lenny in the back seat. I looked in the mirror, but Lenny wasn't paying attention.

"Are you upset?" she asked.

"I'm fine," I said, unwilling to look at her.

I could see her confused face from the corner of my eye. She should know why I was upset. Anyone would have known. Perhaps she wasn't as perceptive as I had initially thought, and I had given her credit for too many things. Maybe that was part of the problem.

I still walked her to homeroom, but I did it in silence. She was going on about something her mom had told her over the weekend, but honestly, I was just trying to focus on putting one foot in front of the other so I could get this part of the morning over with.

I didn't even think about going near her table at lunch, even though I could have easily, especially since Kimberly thought she and I were now dating, but I didn't trust myself, not when I was upset. I could say or do almost anything when I was angry.

"Sit down." Gabe waved me over to the table. He looked as if his head was going to explode.

"You all right, Gabe?"

"You haven't heard?"

I looked at Jackson and Charlie, waiting for an answer, but they weren't saying anything.

"Is someone going to tell me or am I going to have to guess?" I was growing more impatient by the second.

"They found some bodies this morning," Gabe whispered.

My eyes must have looked like they were going to pop out of my head. I hadn't been surprised by anything like that since I got the phone call about my dad.

"Bodies?" I looked at Jackson. He was nodding in agreement. Charlie was doing the same. Immediately, my mind drifted to Old Man Finch. I don't know why I thought of him first. Perhaps something deep inside my conscience still thought he had something to do with those missing teens from Linville.

Gabe held up three fingers.

"The Linville three?" I asked skeptically.

"It has to be," said Jackson. "The police were out there this morning. Apparently, the flood uncovered them."

"Uncovered? Then they didn't find them on the mountain." The water hadn't got anywhere near Finch's place. "So where did they find them?"

"That's the weird part." Gabe leaned in closer. "They found them out in the woods behind Milford's."

"Near the fort?"

"I think so."

"Shit." I suddenly felt cold as I leaned back in my chair. It unnerved me to think we could have stepped over their graves that day in the Alley.

"So what now?" I gathered my thoughts and leaned in toward the center of the table. "Do they have any suspects?"

Gabe shrugged.

"I'm sure they'll have something on the news about it tonight," said Charlie.

Just when I thought things were calming down. The good news was this took my mind off Amanda, which was a blessing.

I rushed home that afternoon and turned on the TV in the living room. WBTV out of Charlotte was carrying the story.

"Earlier today, three bodies were discovered in the woods behind this general store in Evergreen, thirty miles north of Asheville. Authorities say the bodies are so decomposed they'll need to use dental records to identify them. Folks around here are worried they may be the three teenagers who went missing in the fall of 1982 from the neighboring town of Linville. Denise Winters reporting for WBTV."

My pulse raced. I went to my room and looked out the window. Finch's light was on. It had been a few weeks since I'd last seen him. Our chess match had reached a stalemate. If I'd been looking for an excuse to see him, I had one now.

"Mr. Finch!" I knocked furiously on the front door as I reached the cabin. "Mr. Finch, are you in there?" I peered through the window, but the house looked empty. I wondered briefly if the police were interrogating him down at the station, but that thought was quelled when I saw him come staggering to the door.

"Did I wake you?" I noticed the dazed look on his face.

"I like a little cat nap before dinner. Come on in." He rubbed his eyes and opened the door.

"Did you hear about the bodies?" I got straight to it.

He nodded. "Had the news on earlier this afternoon. It's a shame 'bout them kids."

I studied his face carefully. I was 98—no—99 percent sure he had nothing to do with it.

"You think they'll leave me alone now?"

"I hope so. Any idea who might have done it?"

He turned around and looked at me as if I had two heads.

"How the hell should I know?" he asked as he worked himself into his recliner. "Probably an outsider. Someone from Linville or farther down. It happened around the time of the festival so it coulda been anyone. I mean, people come from all over."

He was right. It could have been anyone, and if it wasn't someone from Evergreen, the chances of catching them were remote.

"Any luck in findin' my shotgun?" he asked.

"Afraid not," I answered. "I haven't seen the Rattners since that night. Then with the flood and everything..." My voice fell off.

"It's only a matter of time," he said confidently. "An opportunity will come along sooner or later."

I hoped he was right.

CHAPTER

THIRTEEN

APOCALYPSE

Christmas and New Year were mostly a blur. To my dismay, Amanda spent the entire break in Raleigh visiting her grandparents, but that was probably a good thing from Kimberly's perspective. She was already skeptical of my relationship with Amanda, and I had to go out of my way to reassure her we were only friends. Fortunately, I could be convincing when I needed to be.

Secretly, I talked to Amanda a couple of times over the phone but didn't see her in person for two entire weeks, which was the longest I'd gone without seeing her since we moved to Evergreen. It felt more like an eternity. I even had to wait to give her the Christmas present I bought her, which was a collection of stories from Charles Dickens, her favorite author. I had to go all the way to Asheville to find it.

Mom went overboard with the Christmas decorations, buying wreaths and tinsel and every strand of white lights Milford's had. I was put in charge of climbing the ladder and securing the lights to the gutter, which was difficult considering our roofline. It took an entire afternoon just to get the lights on the house.

Despite having an endless list of chores, the winter break allowed me to spend time with my mom and sister. I had been so busy with school, plotting against Lenny, and chasing after Amanda that I had neglected my family, so we sat down and had dinner every night at the kitchen table and watched Christmas movies and played games like we did in the old days. It was the first time we had done anything like that since moving to Evergreen. The only downside, it made me miss my dad.

My relationship with Kimberly ebbed and flowed like the tide. In the days following the dance, we were with each other twenty-four seven, but after a couple of weeks, the newness wore off, and we argued a lot. Instead of teenagers in love, we acted more like an old married couple. Any problems we had were mostly my fault since there was never a time when my mind was 100 percent on her. I should have done the right thing and broke it off with her, but I was playing a delicate game.

She was Amanda's best friend. I had to keep reminding myself of that. I couldn't treat her too badly, or I'd lose a girlfriend and ruin any chance with Amanda. So I bit my tongue on most occasions and told her whatever she wanted to hear to pacify her.

JANUARY WAS UNEVENTFUL. School resumed, which wasn't bad since we changed classes and Amanda and I now shared art and health. Getting to see her twice every day was both a blessing and a curse, but I tried to make the most of it. When I wasn't thinking about her, I spent a lot of time pondering something Troy Rattner had said in the woods on Halloween night.

He said Mr. Finch was a Watcher, which was a term I hadn't heard before. I became obsessed with finding out what he meant by that. I remembered my grandfather mentioning something about a Watcher in one of the Bible stories he told me as a child, but that had been so long ago the details escaped me.

To educate myself, I began my search in the school library. To my disappointment, it offered little on the subject. Even the library downtown lacked any relevant information aside from a few passages referencing Genesis or the book of Daniel. In fact, to my surprise, there was little on the subject of religion at all. However, I assumed that was mainly because the folks of Evergreen generally considered anything outside *their* way of thinking as blasphemous.

Since I couldn't find anything on my own, I figured the one person who could help was Hal Ridgeway. I knew it was a little risky, but he was a man of the cloth and had gone to seminary in Louisville, so he was educated. I thought if anyone knew about Watchers, it would be him, so I phoned and asked if I could meet with him later that afternoon. He said he was delighted to hear from me and encouraged me to drop by anytime.

I drove out to White Hall after school and parked in the front, near the doors. Hal's car was the only other in the lot, which made me feel better. The last thing I wanted was an audience. It was strange to know the church's doors never closed, but then I remembered the holy spirit doesn't just work on Sunday mornings and Wednesday nights.

As I made my way down the center aisle of the auditorium, it was strange to see it empty, and as I closed my eyes, I could almost hear the residual words of a sermon or a note from "The Old Rugged Cross" echoing through the room. I pushed through a door at the far end, turned left, then climbed a small set of stairs that led to a long hallway. Reverend Ridgeway's office was the first on the left. The door was open, but I knocked anyway. The last thing I wanted was to startle him.

"Brother Cole," he said warmly as he rose from his chair and showed me in.

"Reverend." I shook his hand.

He asked if I would like to sit, and I did. He did the same.

His office was warm and small, but there were hundreds of books on the shelves behind him. Obviously, he was well read or at least gave the appearance he was. This boded well for my chances of finding an answer to my question.

"So what is it you wanted to talk to me about today? There's nothing wrong, is there?"

"No, nothing like that," I reassured him.

"And your mother and sister?"

"Fine as well. Thanks for asking." I paused while I gathered my thoughts. "I heard someone mention something a few weeks ago I had never heard before. I searched all the books in the library but found nothing. I was hoping you could help me."

"I'll certainly do my best." He straightened himself in his chair as curiosity flooded his face.

"I was wondering if you knew anything about Watchers."

The reverend sat up and cleared his throat. "Where did you say you heard this?"

"From a guy at school." I felt terrible for lying in church.

"The term *Watcher* first appears in the book of Genesis," he explained in a professorial voice. There was an open Bible on his desk, so he turned to Genesis and began reading:

And it came to pass, when men began to multiply on the face of the earth, and daughters were born unto them, that the sons of God saw the daughters of men that they were fair; and they took them wives of all which they chose. And the Lord said, my spirit shall not always strive with man, for that he also is flesh: yet his days shall be a hundred and twenty years. There were giants in the earth in those days; and after that, when the sons of God came in unto the daughters of men, and they bore children to them, the same became mighty men which were of old, men of renown.

He looked up at me, but I had difficulty understanding. "Perhaps the book of Daniel is a little easier to digest." As if sensing my confusion, he chose a different verse.

I saw in the visions of my head upon my bed, and behold, a watcher and a holy one came down from heaven.

"So a Watcher is an angel?" I asked, still uncertain whether I had interpreted the passage correctly.

"A fallen angel," he said ominously. "They were thought to have strayed from God and brought unnecessary knowledge to mankind. Of course this is all theoretical. You understand that, don't you?"

"Yes. Of course." I paused. "And what do you think happened to these Watchers... theoretically speaking?"

"Well, I imagine they were rounded up and thrown into the lake of fire after the flood to await Judgment Day."

"So what you're saying is none of them could have

survived, right?"

"Why do you ask?" By the tone of his voice and the look on his face, I could tell that he was growing more suspicious by the second.

"No reason. Just curious."

"I think if the Watchers were real, they would have all been dealt with many generations ago, long before our time."

"So it would be impossible for any to exist today?"

He leaned back in his chair, folded his hands, and let out a hearty laugh.

"Only in the movies, Brother Cole. Only in the movies." He paused. "So how did your mother enjoy the sermon last week?" he asked, changing the subject.

"I think she liked it." I realized that my chance to press him further had passed.

"Can I count on seeing y'all this Sunday?"

"Yes sir. We'll be there."

SUNDAY, FEBRUARY 16, 1986

My seventeenth birthday came and went without much fuss, which is the way I liked it. Mom said I should have had a bigger party, but I told her guys didn't really do that kind of thing, and besides, I thought dinner with the three of us was sufficient. Gabe and Jackson were planning to stay over Friday night, and perhaps Charlie, though he was still trying to decide whether he would ask Sara Finley to a movie. I told him I completely understood if he chose Sara. I would have done the same thing.

Because Mom had gone to the trouble of making my favorite dinner—lasagna—and baking a cake for me, I helped her clean the kitchen. I was finishing sweeping when the doorbell rang.

"I'll get it!" I propped the broom up against the wall, then walked through the living room and crossed the foyer. "Amanda?" I opened the door, surprised to see her. She hadn't been home for days, and I was starting to think she had forgotten about my birthday altogether.

"Hey," she said, raising her gaze to me. She looked glum. "I'm not interrupting, am I?" She peered around me to make sure I didn't have anyone over. I assumed she was looking for Kimberly.

"Of course not. I was sweeping, believe it or not. Do you want to come in?"

"Do you mind if we sit on the porch?"

I grabbed a blanket from the closet and stepped out onto the porch as I shut the door behind me. It was dusk and growing colder by the minute.

We sat down on the swing. The blanket was big enough for the two of us, and I placed it around our shoulders to keep us warm.

"I just got back a few minutes ago and wanted to come by to wish you happy birthday."

"Thanks," I said with a shiver. "I was starting to think you might have forgotten."

She flashed a smile, then looked down as she played nervously with her fingers.

"Did you have a good day?" she asked with a crooked smile, finally looking up.

"Not bad. Mom made lasagna and a chocolate cake."

"Do you feel any different now that you are seventeen?"

I shook my head.

She fell silent again. My gaze drifted to her, but she had turned away.

"Are you... all right?" I was growing more concerned by the second. I had spent enough time around Amanda to know something was off.

She shook her head.

"What's going on?"

I allowed my hand to touch her shoulder softly. She turned and looked up at me for a second, then dropped her gaze. Even in the dying light, I could see tears streaming down her face. She bent forward, burying her head in my chest. I could feel her sobbing convulsively. I felt helpless and didn't know what to do but hold her.

She cried for a long time as I rocked her gently. When her tears stopped, she wiped her face and looked up at me through blurry eyes. I held her a few inches from me as the world around us grew darker.

"I'm sick," she said in a small voice.

Until that moment, I did not know two words had the power to stop your heart. I froze.

It took several seconds before I could find the words. "Sick? I don't understand."

"That's where I've been... at the hospital. All the trips to Raleigh I've been making..."

"To see Ronnie's folks, right?" My words sounded hollow.

She shook her head. "To see the doctors. I didn't want to tell anyone the truth, so I made up the story about Ronnie's parents."

"You could have told me." A feeling of betrayal washed over me, but I stifled it. The strength I was forced to summon to ask the following question took all I had. "How sick are you?" I asked as gently as I could, careful not to upset her further.

Tears welled in her eyes again, and I knew that couldn't be good.

"Sick." She buried her face in her hands.

I felt like I had been sucker punched, and it took several seconds before I could speak again.

"Do the doctors know what it is?" I was trying, unsuccessfully, to wrap my mind around what she was telling me. I was hoping it wasn't something with a long name. Those were always worse.

"Leukemia," she said.

I had heard of it, but admittedly I knew little on the subject and certainly not enough to wager a guess on how serious it was.

"But you don't look sick," I said, trying to be positive.

"I've been sick before," she confessed. "It was a long time ago, before I moved to Evergreen. The cancer's been in remission since I was nine. Honestly, it hadn't crossed my mind in years, but a few months ago I started feeling tired, like before. I knew something didn't feel right. So Mom took me to Raleigh to have tests run, and they confirmed it."

"But you can fight it, right? I mean, you're going to be okay, aren't you?" I felt strange asking her.

"I'm trying to be positive, but I also want to be realistic. The doctor says I have a 30 to 50 percent chance of beating it, but I go back next week for a more accurate prognosis."

I didn't say anything for a long time, mostly because I knew from statistics that anything less than 50 percent was bad. I kept trying to find a ray of hope in this storm of confusion, but so far, there were none. I couldn't imagine how she must be feeling.

"What can I do?" I asked, feeling suddenly tiny. I had

never felt so helpless in my life. My dad's situation was different. It was sudden and final, and there was no time to think about what could be done. Amanda's outcome still hung in the balance, but the odds were not in her favor.

"Just promise to be my friend." She forced a smile. "I need all the support I can get right now."

"Always." I took her hand in mine. "I promise." My words didn't sound like my own. I kept repeating them over and over in my head.

We stayed on the porch for a long time that night without saying a word. She fell asleep with her head on my lap. I had dreamed about such a moment for so long but not like that. I didn't know how much longer I could hold it together. What I felt inside could only be described as a mix of sadness, anger, and confusion.

The following week crawled by, and all I thought about was Amanda. I canceled my date with Kimberly and told her I was sick, but my mind was not in a good place. Mom was worried I was coming down with something, but I told her I was okay. She made me take a dose of cough medicine anyway. I wanted to tell her the truth, but I wasn't ready to have that conversation yet.

After a night of zero sleep, I lumbered my way down into the kitchen on Saturday morning and grabbed a banana and some milk from the fridge and poured a bowl of cereal. I always liked my cereal with fruit, so I sliced the banana and sat down at the table. Mom was already dressed and rushing around looking for her car keys.

"Why the rush?" I shoveled a spoonful of cereal into my mouth.

"I have to go to Charlotte to sign some papers with the

insurance company." She shrugged on her jacket and pulled her hair out from around the collar. "I'll be home later this evening, so if you want to get something from the diner, go ahead. I left a twenty on the counter."

"What about Tabitha?" I inquired, glancing over my shoulder. I spotted the bill hidden neatly within a note, likely explaining all this.

"She's at Darlene's today. I'll pick her up on my way back," she said as she hurried toward the door.

The timing could not have been better. Today was Amanda's follow-up visit with her doctor in Raleigh, and I wanted to make sure I was ready when she got home. I had already decided to go to the library and look up everything I could on leukemia, so as soon as Mom was safely away from the house, I grabbed my jacket and headed out into the cold. A gray sky kept the mood gloomy. I saw that as a bad omen.

I parked the car in the side lot of the library on the off chance someone from school showed up and snuck in through the back door. Privacy was an impossibility in a town as small as Evergreen, and keeping a secret was even harder, so I would need to be careful if I was to be successful.

I gathered an armful of books from the health and medicine section, carried them to a table in the back, and started reading as fast as possible. There were only two other people in the library. One was the librarian; the other was Tom Ellington, the Evergreen Savings & Loan branch manager. He was also a White Hall Baptist Church member, so I tried to keep a low profile.

As I thumbed through the pages, I realized leukemia was essentially blood cancer, which sounded foreboding. But the more I read, I learned that the survival rate was much higher than I had initially expected, depending on the type and severity. For the first time, I felt hopeful.

I could have checked the books out and taken them home to do my research, but I was sure the librarian would have questioned me. Even if I'd been able to convince her it was for another research paper, I'd then have to hide the books at home because if Mom saw them, she would have freaked.

I remembered Amanda saying something about ALL, which was short for acute lymphocytic leukemia, the form most common in children and teens. It said that those who had it as children generally went into remission after eight, but it had little to say about cases where it returned later on.

Rare often meant terrible in the world of medicine. I remember my mom and dad mentioning it years ago when my grandmother got dementia. The speed with which it took her was staggering. She died within a few months of the diagnosis. If I wanted to protect my sanity, those were the kinds of thoughts I needed to keep out of my head. Once you head down the dark road of *what-ifs*, you can't always find your way back.

I made it home around three and waited for Amanda to arrive. The wait was agonizing. Just when I thought I would break, the phone rang. My pulse raced as I lifted the receiver.

"Hey, Kimberly," I said quickly as relief washed over me. I had to walk a bit of a tightrope with her these days. Amanda had made me promise not to say anything.

"Do you know where Amanda is today?" she asked.

"Um, no, I don't. Why, is something wrong?" I wanted to sound genuinely concerned but not too concerned. Kimberly was suspicious about Amanda and me anyway, and I didn't want to do anything to set off alarm bells.

"Just curious," she said. "She's been acting really weird lately. She hasn't said anything, has she?"

Damn. I felt cornered. Kimberly was my—I hated to say it —girlfriend, so I should have been truthful with her, but Amanda and I had a deeper connection—at least I thought so —which meant I couldn't breathe a word of her secret, not even to her best friend.

"No. She hasn't said anything." I was surprised at how easily I could lie to her.

"Hmm. So," she said, changing the subject and brightening her mood, "do you want to get something to eat?"

"Actually, I do," I said, eager to do anything but sit alone in silence. "Give me fifteen minutes. I'll swing by and get you."

I picked up Kimberly, and we drove to the diner, arriving shortly before four. The dinner crowd hadn't arrived yet, which meant a booth was still open. We ordered burgers and fries, and Kimberly wanted a strawberry milkshake, which I gladly paid for. Kimberly was a good friend, though that was all she was ever going to be. Now I just needed to break the news to her.

"Did you hear they finally identified those bodies?"

I looked up from my plate.

"It was those teenagers from Linville—the ones that disappeared a few years ago. Dad says they'll be bringing charges soon."

There was a second and more practical reason I liked Kimberly Davis. Her father was the district attorney, which meant I knew before most others when an arrest would be made. It was just the kind of connection that could come in handy.

"Who are they bringing charges against?" I asked with

sudden interest, careful not to seem too anxious.

"Well, you have to promise not to say anything," she whispered, leaning in. That's what I needed, another secret on my conscience. I'd need to go to church every Sunday from now on to ask God to forgive me for all the sins I'd committed lately. "They're finally going to get Old Man Finch." She appeared happy as she leaned back in her chair and took another drink from the milkshake.

I sat straight up in my chair, not believing what I was hearing. Did she expect me to be happy?

"Cole? Is everything okay?" She reached for my hand, but I pulled away.

"I thought Old Man Finch's name would have been cleared by now. Those bodies weren't found anywhere near the mountain."

She crossed her arms and looked at me through narrow, suspicious eyes. "Why do you care about Old Man Finch so much?" Her guard was up.

"I don't. It's just..."

"Dad has been trying to get him ever since he became DA," she said in a matter-of-fact tone. "He says if he can get him convicted, he'll be on his way to being a judge. Isn't that great?"

I had always thought Kimberly was a decent person, but it appeared the devil was in the details with her.

"And what if he didn't do it?" I offered. "What if your dad is going after the wrong guy?"

"Why would he do that?" She looked annoyed. "If my dad says he did it, then I trust him. Don't you?"

She seemed offended that I had even raised the question, but I didn't care. I knew in my heart Old Man Finch had nothing to do with those murders. Now I would have to find out who did before it was too late.

Rather than continue to anger her, I thought it best to drop the subject. I was going to get nowhere with Kimberly, given the circumstances. Besides, she could give me the inside track on the investigation, which was a line of communication I had to keep open no matter the cost.

"Perhaps you're right." I changed my strategy. "Maybe that old bastard did do it."

A smile broke on her face as I finished the last of my fries.

I dropped Kimberly off at her house at a quarter after five and went straight home. Hopefully, I hadn't missed Amanda. As luck would have it, I could see the blue Chevrolet coming up the street as I pulled into the drive. The butterflies were back. It was like the worst case of stage fright I could imagine times a thousand, and if I had been any older, I would have sworn I was having a heart attack. The car came to a stop, and Amanda got out. Her mom helped her out of the back, put her arm around her, and led her slowly inside. I wasn't an expert on body language, but I didn't get a good feeling.

I went inside and sat in the living room, positioned myself at the end of the sofa where I could see straight to her front door, and waited. Enough time would need to pass before I called. That way, they wouldn't think I was stalking them. Ten... fifteen... twenty minutes went by, and I felt like I was going to explode. As I reached for the phone, I saw her door open. I set the phone back down and watched as she crossed her arms, stepped down off the porch, and began the march toward my house.

It took an eternity for her to reach my front door. My hand was on the door, and I opened it anxiously ahead of her.

I bent my head toward the living room, and she walked in.

"It's just me and you," I told her as I shut the door. "Mom and Tabitha are out and won't be back for a couple of hours."

I grabbed each of us a Coke from the fridge and sat down on the end of the couch, opposite her.

"I went to the library today," I said, breaking the ice. "I've been reading everything I can get my hands on about leukemia." I studied her face carefully.

"I'm dying," she said without looking at me.

I felt like someone had reached inside my chest and ripped out my heart. This was becoming a regular thing with her, only now it was exponentially worse. Neither of us could speak for a very long time. A thousand thoughts raced through my head all at once, none of them positive. All that praying, all that studying, for what? I was angry now, at God, at the world, at life itself, and this time there was no stopping it. She had to say something, or I was going to come unglued.

"The doctor says I have six months at the most." The way she said it, so matter-of-fact, I assumed she was still in shock. Admittedly, so was I.

"So there's nothing they can do?" I was sure she could sense the frustration in my voice.

"They referred me to a doctor in Atlanta, but..." Her voice faded. She had given up. I could see it in her eyes; there was no blue in them today.

When the dam breaks, it doesn't just break a little. My will to be strong was eclipsed by my fear of death—her death—and every fiber of my being ached all at once. I held out as long as I could, but once she started crying, I could no longer resist. I felt her hand fall gently on my shoulder, her head resting against mine, and together we wept.

CHAPTER
FOURTEEN

SACRIFICIAL LAMB

Amanda had only been gone a short time when my mother pulled up in the drive with Tabitha. I felt like running. If I told her what had happened, she would want details, and I didn't have the strength or the patience to describe them to her. Besides, as confused and mad as I was at the moment, there was no way I could endure her interrogation without turning into a monster, so I ran to the only place I could think of where I would be alone.

I went to the overlook and fell to my knees and asked God to take me instead. My fear of heights was subdued for the moment, which made it easier to look down. The town, like my soul, was descending into darkness. I was so transfixed by my sadness I didn't hear footsteps approaching behind me.

"Why are you cryin'?" the voice asked gently.

I looked up and wiped the tears from my eyes. "Mr. Finch? What are you doing here?" I rose to my feet.

"I heard cryin'," he said softly, "so I came to see what was wrong."

It was more than a mile from the overlook to Finch's place. "How did you—?"

"I hear good for an old man." He tugged at his ear as a faint smile appeared. He worked his way to the rock and looked down as the darkness continued its steady march up the mountain. "I've never really been an admirer of heights," he said, peeking over the edge. "But it's quite a view from here, isn't it?"

"You too?" I felt the return of my own fear and inched away from the ledge.

"I used to come here a lot when I was a younger man. The town sure has changed since then." He turned to me and said, "What brings you up here tonight, Cole?" There was a depth of sincerity in his voice I hadn't noticed before.

"My friend, she's sick."

"Cancer?" As if he already knew.

I nodded. I felt the bewilderment on my face.

"I'm sorry. I know how bad cancer can be. That's what took my Martha," he said somberly.

"Mr. Finch, I'm sorry. I didn't know you were married."

"She was a lovely lady, my Martha. She grew up in Montgomery. That's where we met. We had been married just a few years when we moved to Evergreen. Of all the places I've lived in my life, none of them felt like home except this place. There's somethin' about Evergreen—the woods, the trees, the people—that works its way into your heart. You know, sometimes when everyone else has gone to sleep, I come down from the mountain and walk in the woods. I find the trees easier to talk to than people sometimes. Better listeners too."

"You and Amanda would get along," I said, smiling briefly. "You love her, don't you?"

It was one of the few questions he asked that I didn't have to dwell on. "With all my heart."

"I know that look. That's the same look I had when Martha was around. I take it by you being here her diagnosis isn't good."

My smile faded. "No, it isn't. The doctors are telling her six months."

Mr. Finch sat for a long time, staring out into the trees before speaking again.

"You was up here prayin', wasn't you?" he asked, looking troubled.

I nodded. "Not sure what good it'll do though. My mom prayed for my dad all the time and look what happened to him."

"Not all prayers are answered, you know. Sometimes bad things happen just because they do. That's life. If everyone had their prayers answered, what kind of world would that be?"

"I suppose you're right." I watched the shadow below as it crept closer. "I went to see Reverend Ridgeway a few weeks ago. When the Rattners had Lenny tied to the tree that night, I heard one of them say you were a Watcher." I gauged his reaction.

He let out a chuckle. "I've been called many names." He looked straight ahead as the light from the sun blazed in his eyes.

"Does that mean you're not—a Watcher, I mean?" That had been eating away at me for so long I had to know the answer.

"What do you think? What does your heart tell you?"

"I don't know," I said, feeling bewildered. I studied his face, searching for an answer. His appearance differed from before, younger again. Maybe it was my imagination. Exhaustion can play funny tricks on the mind, and I was plenty tired. "No offense, but you look like an old man to me."

He chuckled again, this time louder. "None taken." After a few seconds, the smile faded. "There's something you want to ask me, isn't there?"

"You know things, don't you?"

He didn't respond right away, but after a while, he nodded slowly. "You don't get to be as old as I am without learning a few things along the way."

"But it's more than that, isn't it?" I probed. "You know things before they happen. How?"

He turned and stared at me with those cold eyes for an immeasurable amount of time. So long, in fact, I almost withdrew my question, but I remained resolute. I had to know.

He set his gaze upon the horizon again. "The mysteries of the universe are hidden from every man. Some, if they're lucky, get a glimpse now and then, but most can't see the bigger picture. They're too busy livin' their lives to notice, and I suppose that's the way God intended it to be. When I was just a little fella, my mama would tell everyone I was her *special* boy. She knew there was somethin' in me that was different. I'd wander around in them woods all day long, just starin' up at the trees, listenin' to the wind. That's when I heard the voices for the first time. They used to whisper in my ear and tell me things."

His words made the hair on the back of my neck stand on end.

"What kinds of things?"

"Things that hadn't happened yet." I could feel his eyes on me now, but I didn't want to look at him because I was thinking of Amanda and the dream she'd had. She could see things too. "When I got a little older, other mysteries were revealed to me."

"Then you are a Watcher."

He looked at me again. "Like I said, I've been called many things.

"Then if you know things before they happen, tell me what happens to Amanda," I begged. "Does she survive? Can she beat the cancer?"

He thought about my question for a long time, then told me what he saw. "There are two paths I see—one is life, the other—" His voice fell off as he dropped his gaze.

There was the bewilderment again. I felt so helpless. "Can you help her?"

"No, but you can." He looked at me with those eyes again.

"Me? How can I help?"

He put his arm around me and patted me on the back. "Try prayin' first."

"And if that doesn't work?"

He let out a long sigh. "If prayin' don't work, come see me again, and we'll talk about it. For now, it's gettin' late, and you look like you've had a very long day. Go on home and rest. I see a time comin' when you're gonna need every ounce of strength you can muster. It'll snow tonight. Wait until the third day, then pay me a visit. We still have a game that needs finishin'."

I did as Mr. Finch suggested and went straight home, leaving him at the overlook as darkness fell over Evergreen.

That night I was plagued by strange dreams, though I struggled to remember the details when I woke in the morning.

As I opened my eyes, I could tell by the light in the room something was different. It was a hazy blue I knew all too well. "Snow." I sat up in bed. I went to the window, and sure enough, everything was covered in a blanket of white. Finch had been right. Suddenly, I felt cold.

I went to wake Tabitha because I knew how much she loved the snow, but she wasn't in her room. She and Mom were already downstairs eating breakfast, their snow gear laid across the back of the sofa.

"It snowed," I announced gladly as I made my way into the kitchen.

"I know," Mom said. "Tabby and I are going out after breakfast. Do you want to join us?"

"I'll think about it." I filled a plate with sausage, biscuits, and eggs. To my surprise, there was a bowl of gravy sitting at the end of the counter, so I smothered everything on my plate in it.

Now that the excitement of the snow was wearing off, the exhaustion came flooding back. I didn't realize what an emotional toll Amanda's situation was taking on me.

I needed to sleep, but my mind said to get out of the house and enjoy the fresh air. Amanda was home, but I didn't know if she felt like company today or not. Any doubts I might have had were erased as I looked out the window and saw her building a snowman. I put on my snow pants and jacket, got my toboggan, and stepped out into the world of white.

I wasn't sure how to act around her because I didn't know

how she was feeling. "Are you okay this morning?" I asked delicately.

"I'm not dead yet," she joked, though I didn't appreciate the humor.

"You want some company? I'm kind of an expert at snowman building."

"Sure."

That morning, under the falling snow, Amanda and I built the biggest snowman I had ever seen. It must have been at least seven feet tall. We grabbed some Oreos from the kitchen, made eyes and a carrot for a nose, and made Cindy take a picture with her Polaroid. Amanda said I could keep it as something to remember her by. She always had a way of saying things like that at the worst time.

She invited me in for hot chocolate, which I happily accepted, and we sat by the fire talking while Cindy went about vacuuming the upstairs.

"This is the first time I've been in your house," I said as my eyes scanned the room.

It wasn't huge, but it was comfortable. The room was painted an eggshell white, and there was a piano in the corner and a large cream-colored sofa that sat in front of the TV. Cindy Davenport was a lot of things, but messy wasn't one of them. I had never seen a house as put together as that one. There wasn't a thing out of place. She also loved to take pictures, and there were dozens of them all over the living room.

"Really? Are you sure?" she asked.

"Positive."

"I guess you're right," she admitted. She took me by the

hand and pulled me from the sofa. "In that case, let me show you my room."

We turned right at the top of the stairs. Her room was at the end of the hall. It was painted lilac, and she had two windows, one that looked in the direction of the cul-de-sac, the other down the hill toward James Street. I could see Lenny's house easily from here.

"Remember the first day we met?" she asked as she opened the window to let the cold air rush in.

"Of course I remember. You were trying to get away from your mom."

"And you were so nervous."

"Was not. Okay, maybe a little, but it was only because..." I stopped just short of saying it, but it had been her that made me nervous. She was so beautiful that day on the porch. She still was.

She turned to me. "Because of what?"

"It's not important. What are all these?" I quickly changed the subject as I examined the pictures she kept in wooden frames on top of her dresser.

"My closest friends," she said with a sigh. "That's me and my friend Destiny at the beach, and there's Rachel, Michelle, and Wendy that time we went to Six Flags, and Kimberly of course."

That one must have been taken when they were ten or eleven. I almost didn't recognize Kimberly with braces and freckles. At the end of the dresser was the picture of us from the day we went to church together. Now that I looked at it, I realized she had been right; we matched. It did my heart good not to see a picture of Rusty anywhere.

"So how are things with you and Kimberly?" She took a

seat at the end of the bed. "With everything going on, it's hard to keep up."

"We fight a lot." I eased myself into a chair near the closet. "Mom thinks it's because we like each other so much, but..."

"You don't agree?"

"Kimberly's a great girl, and I know you two are best friends. But she's just..."

"Not the one?" she asked, flashing her eyes at me.

"Exactly."

From the corner of my eye, I thought I saw the hint of a smile in the corner of her mouth, but by the time I really looked, it was gone.

"What about you?"

It took her a second to respond, as if she were lost in a daydream. "What?"

"You and Rusty?" It pained me to say his name.

She let out a sigh. "I broke it off." She was playing nervously with her fingers again. "After I knew I was sick, I figured why lead him on? Besides, graduation is coming up, and he'll be off to NC State soon. He says he's leaving early so he can start practicing with the team."

"I'm sorry," I said, though not an ounce of me would be sorry to see him go.

"I'm sorry too... about you and Kimberly," she said. "I feel responsible since I was the one who set you up." She looked down again.

"Don't be sorry. Sometimes you just have to strike out a few times before the right person comes along."

Her gaze drifted to mine, and there was something different now; I could feel it, but she looked away quickly as my heart sped up. She got up slowly, went to the window, and looked out as the cold air rushed in. The glow of the snow cast her face in a pale hue, and for a moment, I thought she looked more dead than alive. It made me shiver.

"Do you think there's a chance I can beat this?" she asked, staring out into the world of white. Her tone was serious now.

A million thoughts raced through my head at once, but I remembered what Finch had told me the night before.

"I do," I said earnestly, though if I was honest with myself, I couldn't be sure, not 100 percent sure.

"I want to beat this," she said desperately, "more than anything I've ever wanted in my life. There are so many things I want to do, so much I want to experience..." Her voice fell off, and as if propelled by some unseen force, I rose from the chair and went to where she was standing. Any trepidation melted away, leaving only determination. My hands fell gently upon her shoulders. She was trembling.

She turned to me, and I stared into her eyes. They were blue again, just like the first time I saw her, but there was also sadness—a deep, consuming sadness.

"Cole, I—"

"Shh," I whispered softly. We had been building to this moment for months, and nothing was going to stand in the way now. I brushed back the hair from her eyes and took her face in my hands and held it gently, as if it were made of the most fragile porcelain. My eyes never left hers. Her skin was unimaginably soft, unbelievably perfect.

Firmly but gently, I drew her closer and watched breathlessly as she closed her eyes and let out a sigh. When I kissed her, I knew she was the one I wanted to spend the rest of my life with. I kissed her again, and this time she kissed me back, softly, tenderly, and for a moment, the entire world vanished, taking with it our troubles.

"I love you, Amanda." I gazed intently into her eyes. "I've loved you from the first moment I saw you."

She kissed me again. I supposed it was her way of saying she loved me too.

We stayed in her room until late in the afternoon, talking and laughing, and for the first time since she told me her cancer had returned, I was hopeful. I knew then I had to find a way for her to live.

It took three days for the snow to melt, just like Finch said it would. When I got to the top of the mountain, I saw him sitting on the porch in the rocking chair.

I called out as I approached, "You'll freeze to death out here."

"Not in the sunlight, my boy." He grinned broadly. He was in a good mood today, and I was in the best mood. "I love the cold on a winter's morning." He drew in a long breath before he rose to his feet. "It has a way of refreshing the soul. You hungry?"

"I could eat." I'd been in such a hurry to see him I had forgotten breakfast.

We went inside where it was warm. He had a fire going, a big, roaring fire. The smell of bacon hung in the air, and there was a pan of biscuits cooling on the table.

"I got eggs too if you want," he said as he sat down at the table.

I told him to eat, and I'd take care of the eggs. I scrambled the few that were left in the carton and set them on the table. Finch was mildly surprised I knew my way around the kitchen, but I had picked up a few tricks from my dad.

"I've been thinking about our match." I opened a biscuit and doused it with honey.

"Yeah? What about it?"

"What do you think is the riskiest move someone can make?"

"Hmm." He seemed intrigued by my question. "The King's Gambit is the riskiest opening, but if we're talkin' single moves, it has to be sacrificin' your queen." He stared at me for a long time. "It's the most versatile piece on the board. Without it, victory is damn near impossible and not something I would recommend."

When we finished eating, we made our way back to the board. It was his move.

He pushed his bishop to g1, capturing my rook. He flashed a smile. I advanced the center pawn, then his queen took my second rook.

"Check." He looked both relieved and concerned.

I studied the board carefully, then moved my king out of harm's way.

He looked at me, then back to the board. "Tell me, Cole, how is Amanda doing?"

"Hard to say. Some days she seems like her old self, and others she can hardly get out of bed. I suppose it's the medicine that makes her feel so bad."

"Did you try prayin' like I asked?"

I told him I had, which wasn't a lie because I had prayed every night since we last spoke. "But like I said before, I don't see how it's going to help."

"Let's give it a little more time, hmm? It takes time for prayers to work. You can't pray in the mornin' and expect an answer in the afternoon."

"No. I suppose not. I'll try anything at this point. I just want her to be all right."

"Anything?" He looked up and flashed a wicked smile—one I hadn't seen since the first time we met.

"Yes, anything. Why? What are you thinking? You have an idea, don't you?"

"Maybe." He rubbed his chin. "Oh, I been meanin' to ask you..." Oh so elegantly, he changed the subject. "How's the hunt comin' for my shotgun? You ever seen them Rattner boys?"

"No," I said miserably, "but I'm going to take care of that very soon. Like I told you, I'll get that gun back." Seizing on an opportunity, I advanced the knight, flanking his king.

"Check." I felt the corners of my mouth curl into a smile.

"Don't gloat," he said as if he knew what I was thinking.

I wasn't sure if he realized it, but he had sealed his fate two moves prior. Admittedly, I had only come to the same conclusion. I'd already considered all the possibilities and knew the game would soon be over. Now it was only a matter of time.

CHAPTER
FIFTEEN

VENGEANCE

For days, I savored Finch's impending doom. We had been at this game for months, and I was ready for it to be over so I could focus on more important matters. I gathered all Amanda's work from school and helped her with it in the evenings to pass the time. She told me I would make an excellent teacher someday, which I appreciated, though I figured she was mostly trying to be nice.

After our breakthrough, we kissed pretty much whenever we saw each other, and our love blossomed. It did my heart good to know the feelings I'd harbored for so long were not in vain. I missed not being able to take her to school, but Lenny kept me company. It was a shame he and I hadn't gotten off to a better start, because he was actually a decent guy. He even talked about going on to college and had dreams of opening a flower shop someday. Go figure.

It would have been ungentlemanly of me to defeat Finch in chess without first returning his shotgun, so I was glad we stopped when we did. But it would only take one more visit to finish the game, which meant I had to steal the gun back from the Rattners sooner rather than later. Defeating an old man in a chess match was one thing, but the Rattners were altogether different. To get Finch's shotgun back would require me to play a game where there were no rules and most certainly no gentlemen.

If Evergreen was the size of a postage stamp, the town of Norma was a speck. Situated along the Calloway River, Norma, which was nothing more than a dozen or so rusted-out mobile homes huddled around what had at one time been a pool hall, lay between Evergreen and Linville at the end of a dirt road off Highway 221. It was widely known that Tommy and Troy Rattner spent most of their time in Linville since it was only a few miles away and would only wander into Evergreen when they were looking for trouble.

Jackson, Gabe, Lenny, and I had a bone to pick with the Rattners, and we knew the only way we were going to get back at them for what they had done was to catch them off guard. So under cover of darkness, the four of us jumped in my car and made the drive to Norma. It was cold that night, much colder than it had been all winter. Tiny flakes of snow danced on my windshield as I killed the lights and pulled off on the side of the gravel road.

"Stop here," said Lenny, looking nervous. His hands shook so badly I thought about Mr. Franklin, the ninety-year-old man who had lived beside us in Rochester. He had Parkinson's and shook like a leaf all the time.

I turned off the engine, and the four of us climbed out of the car and into the cold still night. We could see lights at the bottom of the hill from where we stood, twinkling like stars in a vast universe of darkness.

"W-which one is it?" asked Jackson, shivering from the cold.

"Third one from the left," said Lenny, who had stopped shaking and was looking resolute.

Tommy and Troy Rattner lived in that rusted aluminum box with their cousin Eddie Lowe, a twenty-nine-year-old convicted felon who had been sentenced to ten years in the state pen for aggravated robbery when he was nineteen. He was known throughout Avery County as the meanest, most vile son of a bitch you'd ever want to run across, and most people said he'd rather shoot you than look at you. There were rumors he had killed a man on a hunting trip when he was only sixteen, but no one had ever found the body. In that part of the world, the saying *no body, no crime*, was the God's honest truth, so he was never convicted.

We kept to the side of the road, careful not to make our presence known. I knew that folks around here protected their own, so if anyone knew we were there, the whole place would be on us like a pack of wild dogs. I shuddered to think what would happen if we were caught.

The whole time I was descending the hill, my thoughts drifted from the Rattners to Kimberly and then to Amanda. Admittedly, I'd gotten caught up in the moment at the dance in December, but it was nothing like the kiss I shared with Amanda. It felt like it had taken a lifetime to get there with her, and the mature thing to do was tell Kimberly.

It's funny the way fear affects your behavior. As we

descended in silence, I thought about how rare it was for any of the four of us to be quiet for longer than five seconds, and yet here we were, tight-lipped, dead silent, five minutes and counting.

When we reached the bottom of the hill, gravel lanes fanned out in several directions. We chose the path on the left that led toward three trailers that sat apart from the others. Though they were separated by a hundred feet, they were still close enough so that if anyone yelled, everyone could hear them.

I was shocked these homes hadn't been lifted off their cinder block foundations and swallowed by the flood. They could just as easily have been carried downstream, probably dammed up at the old Creekmill Bridge, the one that crossed the river above Pineola. I supposed even God had pity on the wicked sometimes.

First things first, we needed to know if the Rattners and their cousin were at home. Things could get messy if a fight broke out, and although we had them outnumbered, I feared it was a fight we couldn't win. We ducked into the bushes off the side of the road and climbed up a small hill to where we could see through the windows. Going through the icy under-brush was tough, and I thought about bears again, though it now felt more like we were the bears. The house appeared empty at first, then something moved in front of the light.

"Eddie," whispered Lenny, speaking for the first time in what seemed like an hour.

I glanced at Jackson and Gabe. Jackson had a look of deter-mination on his face, but Gabe was his usual scared self, though since he had started dating Marie Helton, he was infinitely more confident than when I first met him.

"You guys ready for this?" I looked mainly at Gabe.

They nodded resolutely.

Turning my eyes back to the trailer, I thought of Amanda again. What would she think of us—of me—out here in the freezing cold, minutes away from taking part in my second robbery? I tried to push it out of my head.

"I think he's alone." Lenny fixed like a hawk on the open window. "What do you want to do?"

I had no intentions of confronting anyone if I didn't have to. Fortunately, while I was thinking about it, Eddie received a phone call. We could see him talking, soundless, through the window. A few minutes later, he left in a rush, speeding up the hill, spitting gravel as he went. I hoped we had hidden the car well enough so he would notice.

"Okay." I stood up. "Let's go."

We slipped out of the trees and found the front porch. The door was unlocked, which didn't surprise me. I told the others to stay low. I didn't want any of the neighbors to look in and see us going through the place. Otherwise, we'd never see the light of day again.

"Let's get the shotgun and get out of here." I sent Jackson and Gabe to one end while Lenny and I searched the other.

I rifled through a closet, and Lenny poked his head into one of the bedrooms, but there was so much trash lying around it was a bit of a needle-in-a-haystack situation.

"Anything?" I asked Lenny.

He shook his head.

"Wait." He seemed to spot something off in one of the bedrooms. He disappeared around the corner, then came back with a small box. It looked like junk to me at first, maybe some things they had stolen during one of their robberies, but the longer I looked at it, I noticed there were IDs, a checkbook from a bank in Asheville, and an assortment of keys. There were other items, but I didn't have time to study them all because Jackson and Gabe were back in the living room holding the shotgun.

"All right, we got what we came for." I felt triumphant. "Now let's get out of here." No sooner had the words left my mouth than headlights appeared through the window.

The four of us froze where we stood.

"Shit," said Gabe, his go-to phrase when he panicked.

"Damn, damn, damn," said Jackson, the first of us to move. He darted for the back door and eased it open.

We all crept out the back. I was last to leave. We had just made it out as Eddie came back through the front door with Tommy and Troy. They looked drunk or high or both, but their eyes were red, and they were slurring their speech as they searched for more beer.

"Shit," I said, mostly to myself as I peered in through the tiny window in the door. I watched their faces, hoping they wouldn't realize someone had been inside. How could they, with all the trash lying around?

I slipped off the back porch and found the guys waiting at the corner. We went back the way we had come, across the driveway and into the woods. We were ready to make a break for the car when the front door swung open. It was Tommy Rattner. If looks could kill, we would have all been dead that night. I watched his eyes peer out into the forest, and for a second, I swore he could see us. His eyes were black as night and full of rage. I suppose it's true what they say about some people being born evil. If there was ever any doubt, the Rattners were living proof of it. I had never seen the guys that still in my life, frozen like statues. I don't think any of us took a breath for a whole minute.

Just then, Troy came around one corner of the house with Eddie around the other, and soon the three of them stood in the front yard only thirty feet from us.

"They have to be close," Eddie muttered, low and menacing.

I looked at the guys. Fear was creeping into their gaze, but I instructed them to remain still.

Watching Eddie and the Rattners, I thought about my comic books, strangely enough. It was perhaps the most dangerous moment of my life. A few months back suddenly felt like a lifetime ago.

We watched the three of them run to a neighbor's trailer and knock on the front door. It was our chance to get out of there. We slipped off the side of the hill, careful not to make too much noise though the ground was frozen, and everything crunched frostily beneath our feet.

When we reached the foot of the big hill, I jumped in front and led the way, careful to stay at the edge of the trees in case someone came up the gravel road. My heart raced as we made the ascent, and I glanced over my shoulder with every other step to make sure they weren't following us.

We climbed into the car and started the engine. It was the only time I wished I didn't have a sports car because it let out a growl I was sure everyone at the bottom of the hill could hear. I tore out of there as fast as I could and never looked back.

As soon as we charged onto Highway 221, the car erupted in triumphant—and relieved—shouts and cheers.

When we made it to Evergreen, I dropped off Jackson and

Gabe, then took Lenny back to James Street. The porch light was on when we got there.

"I couldn't have done it without you," I said to Lenny. "I think we make better friends than enemies, don't you?"

"Couldn't agree more," he said, then his tone turned serious and thoughtful. "Cole, can I ask you something?"

"Sure."

"You've been out there in the world. Do you think I could make it outside a place like this?"

His question caught me off guard, and I took a few seconds to consider it properly. Whenever I thought of Evergreen, I thought about Lenny Sanders and vice versa. They, like New York and the Big Apple, were inextricably linked.

"I think anything is possible," I replied, careful not to dissuade him.

"Even for someone like me?"

"Especially for someone like you. You're a good guy, Lenny. Don't let anyone tell you otherwise."

"Thanks," he said as he climbed out of the car. "Oh, by the way. My dad enrolled in an AA program in Linville. I think it's really helping. Tell your mom I said thanks." And with that, Lenny Sanders was gone.

When I got home, my mom was asleep on the couch with Tabitha in her arms. I didn't have the heart to wake them, so I grabbed the quilt from the back of the sofa and placed it gently over them, then turned off the TV and climbed the stairs to my room. I sat down on the end of the bed and thought about how lucky the four of us had been that night. It wasn't often I was terrified, but now that the adrenaline was wearing off, I was certain we had escaped death by the skin of our teeth. I knew there would be retaliation, but that could wait until morning.

———

THE SOUND of bacon frying in a pan was like music to my ears. I woke to that unmistakable salty smell, which I had grown fond of since moving to Evergreen. My feet hit the cold floor, and it brought a shiver. Outside, the world was frosty, everything encapsulated in ice crystals that glittered like diamonds. I got dressed and made my way downstairs to an unusual and unexpected scene. My mother was standing at the door talking to Chief Morris. The first thing that ran through my mind was the shotgun. I'd been in such a rush to get home I forgot all about it being in the car.

I froze where I stood and waited for the news as Mom shut the door. She turned around and found me at the top of the stairs. The look on her face was not one of anger but of sadness.

"What is it?" I asked as a feeling of uneasiness swelled inside me.

She couldn't speak for a few seconds, and the longer it went on, the more my mind conjured dark thoughts.

"It's Lenny."

"What about Lenny?" I asked nervously.

"Cole, he's dead," she said in a labored voice.

My heart stopped. It took at least a minute for my brain to restart, though it might have been longer. Time stands still in situations like that. My face must have looked distorted because I could feel my brow pressing down against my eyes.

Numbness spread through my entire body as I eased myself into a sitting position on the stairs.

I shook my head slowly for a few more seconds before finding words. "I just saw him last night." My first thought was Carl had something to do with this, but that theory quickly evaporated as Mom relayed the details.

"Chief Morris said they found..." Her voice broke off. She covered her mouth with her hand as if trapping the words, which meant what she had to say next carried with it a heavy burden. "He said they found Lenny this morning... hanging from a tree in his backyard."

It was too awful to wrap my mind around. That wasn't the work of Carl Sanders. It was the work of Tommy and Troy Rattner and their cousin Eddie. The devastation was quickly replaced by anger so complete I could do nothing to stop it from taking over. Just then I thought about Lenny's father. How had this happened while he was at home?

"What about Carl? Where was he while this was happening?" I asked angrily.

"Linville." Mom buried her head in her hands. "I introduced him to Travis Comber. He's a friend of mine who runs the AA group at the convention center. That's where Carl was last night. It was his first meeting."

The pain I now felt was like nothing in my life. I'd let Evergreen get under my skin, and I hated myself for it. I made a promise right then and there to Lenny and to God that Tommy, Troy, and Eddie would all pay for what they had done.

Word of Lenny's death spread through Evergreen like wildfire. By noon, everyone knew he was dead and what had happened to him. The school had already announced they would hold a candlelight vigil in the parking lot that evening from seven to eight for anyone who wanted to come out and pay their respects. Amanda was beside herself with grief.

I had to get away, so I went up on the mountain, lugging that godforsaken shotgun with me, using every curse word I could think of, even the ones I'd heard other people say but never dared to say myself. I thought about burning the damn thing or tossing it off the side of the mountain, but it carried with it now the burden of Lenny's soul. It was a symbol of death and destruction, and I wanted nothing more than to return it to Finch and never see it again.

As I thought about it more, there were many things I wished—for my dad and Lenny to still be alive, for Amanda to not be sick, and for the Rattners and their cousin to be six feet deep in a hole somewhere. I would gladly sacrifice the three of them to save Amanda from her fate and even asked God to make it so. Amanda was right; life was not fair.

"He's dead!" I burst through the door and thrust the shotgun into Finch's hands. "Lenny Sanders is dead." I went around him and stopped before I made it to the living room.

"The Rattners?"

I nodded.

"There're only a few folks round here capable of somethin' like that. Not a good bone in any of them."

"I want them dead!" I said harshly, hardly able to contain my rage. "All of them."

"I know how you're feeling." He offered me a seat at the kitchen table and propped the gun up against the clock in its usual place. "But they'll get what's comin' to them, trust me. Where them boys is goin', no man wants to follow. But you can't take it upon yourself to be judge, jury, and executioner, even for insignificant nothin's like the Rattners."

His words did little to assuage my anger. I sat in silence for a long time. Finch got up and made a skillet of biscuits and fried some ham and eggs and sat down to eat. He offered me a plate, but I wasn't hungry.

"What should I do?" I asked when I could speak calmly.

"It's in God's hands now... and the police. Let the chief do his job, but if he asks, you'll have to tell him what you was doin' there last night."

I had been so angry over Lenny's death that I hadn't thought about what it meant for me. "No." I could get in big trouble over this whole thing. "I can't go to the chief. It's too late for that."

"It's never too late to tell the truth." Finch chewed on a bite of ham.

"But what if I get in trouble—and Jackson and Gabe?" I asked desperately, thinking now of the consequences. "We were all there last night." I could see all three of us sharing a cell down at the jail. They might take it easy on Gabe and Jackson since they were from here. Me, on the other hand... I shuddered to think of what they might do to me. It might be like those Salem witch trials. I could smell the fire now.

"A young man is dead," Finch said bluntly, fixing his gaze on me, the last piece of ham resting at the end of his fork. "Besides, you've done nothin' wrong, and if Chief Morris asks me, I'll tell him Troy or Tommy were the ones that robbed me."

"I appreciate that, but I'm not sure how much pull you have with Chief Morris these days. They still think you had something to do with the deaths of those kids from Linville. And what if they find out we broke into their place last night?

They'll lock us up for that, even if it was to take back something they stole."

He stopped and stared at me with cold eyes.

"The time is comin' when you must make some tough decisions. Sounds to me like you got some more prayin' to do." He went back to his breakfast.

———

WE BURIED Lenny Sanders on a Tuesday beneath a miserable gray sky. I suppose it was fitting, considering he was that way most of the time—miserable, that is. Behind the tough exterior, there was something sad about Lenny. He was one of those souls who had the misfortune of being around broken people, and thus he became broken himself. Even God shed tears for Lenny Sanders that day.

The town cemetery had headstones dating back as far as 1792, which was much older than I expected. There was even one, though weathered to the point where the name was hardly visible, of a man from Evergreen who had fought in the Revolutionary War. It sat in a green pasture behind the White Hall Baptist Church and was surrounded by a fence made of iron.

The lot was packed that morning, and it looked like the entire town had come out to wish Lenny well as he passed from this life to the next. I supposed Lenny was known by all for one thing or another, good or bad. Maybe it was like that for everyone who lived in a small town. As I walked up the narrow path that led to his final resting place, I kept thinking about what he said to me when he got out of the car that night, about whether he could make it outside a place like

Evergreen. It was almost as if he knew what was going to happen. It was only then, amid the numbing pain and confusion, that I regretted everything I had done to Lenny.

Almost everyone from school was there too, including Derek and Ricky, who cried as much as anyone I had ever seen. It was strange to see people when they were hurting, as if the facade they had worked so diligently to build was suddenly stripped away, leaving behind a nucleus of frailty.

Amanda was there, of course, but she kept her distance. Kimberly was there too and was draped all over me like an old coat. I felt guilty with her in my arms when my thoughts were elsewhere. The dark side Amanda alluded to that first weekend seemed prophetic now, and I wondered if, in the end, it would be the side that emerged victorious in the battle raging inside me.

As expected, Reverend Ridgeway performed the funeral and had prepared some pleasant words to say about Lenny. He spoke from the book of Isaiah:

The righteous perish, and no one takes it to heart; the devout are taken away, and no one understands that the righteous are taken away to be spared from evil.

Those who walk uprightly enter into peace; they find rest as they lie in death.

Carl was there too, looking like the weight of the world was on his broad, slumping shoulders. He cried like a baby. Seeing a grown man cry was unnerving. I don't think I ever saw my father shed a tear, not even when Grandpa died. I always thought that was a sign of strength, but now I questioned his humanity after this. I was too numb to cry and feel much of anything, really, except anger and despair.

When it was over, the crowd bled away. Kimberly stayed

with me for a while but went home with her mom and dad and said she'd call me later. I remained long after the crowd dispersed. The thought of Lenny alone in the cold was too much for me to comprehend. Amanda stayed too, and eventually, it was just the two of us, sitting silently as the rain beat down on the roof of the green tent above us.

I wanted to tell her what had happened, but I couldn't; she wouldn't understand. I sat there and held her while she shed a few more tears and told me funny stories about Lenny from when they were younger. Thank God Kimberly had left, or otherwise, she would have had come apart. I wanted to tell her about Amanda and me, but Amanda wouldn't let me, at least not yet. She said she wanted to wait to see if her cancer would go away before I ruined my chances with Kimberly.

That night, I thought about Lenny a great deal, the first day in homeroom when he called me out in front of everyone, the day I saw him take a beating from his dad, the day in the woods, and the night at the festival. My emotions had run the gamut with him, making his loss even more painful to live with. It was the first time in a long time I wished I was back in Rochester. Nothing like this ever happened there, where it was uneventful, monotonous, and above all, safe.

CHAPTER

SIXTEEN

CROWN OF THORNS

It took two months to come out of the fog I had been in since Lenny died. His death had affected me more than I was willing to admit. Reverend Ridgeway offered to counsel anyone who felt like they needed it, so I took him up on the offer and visited him a couple of times at his office. Despite my trepidation, he shared some words of wisdom that helped with the grieving. I wished he had been there when my dad died.

The day after Lenny's funeral, Chief Morris arrested the Rattners and their cousin Eddie and charged them with murder. Under North Carolina law, they stood to get the death penalty, which seemed only fair—an eye for an eye, that's what the Good Book says. The way I saw it, those bastards got what they deserved, just like Finch said they would. I was starting to realize he was wiser than I gave him credit for.

But the bad news seemed to outweigh the good. Amanda had been getting progressively worse, which meant she spent more time in the hospital and less time in Evergreen. Against her wishes, I finally broke it off with Kimberly. I had a dark side, but I wasn't a complete monster. It wasn't fair to keep going on as if I liked her when I didn't, and besides, the more she went on about her father pursuing Mr. Finch, the more I wanted to be as far away from her as possible. Thaddeus Finch was a good man, and he was my friend, but when it came to his innocence, Kimberly was clearly on one side while I was on the other.

Despite our differences, she had been right about one thing. Her father would not stop until he had Mr. Finch behind bars. On the last Saturday in April, as I got ready to start my day, I went into the living room and turned on the TV. To my surprise, there was Mr. Finch, being led off the mountain in handcuffs. Robert Davis looked as happy as a lark, standing in for interviews in his three-piece suit, hair slicked back, a greedy smile stretched across his face.

I threw on my jacket and jumped into the car. Usually, I would go to Amanda, but she had taken a turn for the worse and was at the hospital in Raleigh full-time now. I set out to find Gabe and Jackson. They would know what to do. I phoned Gabe, but his mom said he and Jackson had just left for the diner, so I jumped in the car and sped off toward town.

"I guess you heard?" asked Jackson as I walked in and sat down at the booth.

Rhonda looked up from behind the counter. "Hey, honey, can I getcha anything?"

"Coke please," I said, then turned to them. "Yeah, I heard. So what are we going to do?"

"We?" Gabe looked disgusted, as though I had asked him

216

to commit a crime. "Have you forgotten what happened the last time we did something?"

"And it's going to end the same way if we do nothing," I replied.

"What are you talking about?" Jackson asked.

"Before Kimberly and I broke up, she told me if her dad arrested Finch, he was going to get the death penalty for him. The only reason that son of a bitch is doing it is so he can become a judge."

"But if he did it, then I agree with Mr. Davis," said Gabe.

The whole time Gabe and I had been friends, I couldn't remember a time when we'd had even the slightest disagreement, but I guess there's a first time for everything. "You know as well as I do Old Man Finch had nothing to do with those murders."

"Then who was it?" asked Jackson.

Rhonda appeared and sat the Coke down in front of me. I thanked her, and she returned to the kitchen. I shifted slowly from Gabe to Jackson. "I think it was the Rattners. After what they did to Lenny, it's obvious they're capable. Do you really think Lenny was their first?" I'd had plenty of time to think about it, and given their propensity for violence and total disregard for life, they were the only logical choice. Besides, that first encounter with them when we were at the old fort had puzzled me. I suspected now that they were there to move the bodies. My question hung in the air for several long seconds before they said anything.

"Shit." Jackson leaned back in his seat. "You may be right. But how are you going to prove it? And wouldn't the police have found something tying them to the crime? I heard there was nothing left of the place when the cops got finished with it."

"I don't know," I said. Jackson had a good point. If the Rattners had done it, the police should have found something.

"Maybe they *did* find something," Gabe said. "If you're right—and I'm not saying you are—what if they found evidence and Mr. Davis had them hide it?"

On the surface, that Robert Davis would have suppressed evidence just to get a conviction seemed preposterous. Still, when men get greedy or desperate, they'll do almost anything. I couldn't discount the idea altogether.

I didn't say anything to Jackson or Gabe, but in the back of my mind, I still wasn't 100 percent sure Mr. Finch was a good guy. He appeared to be harmless, but now and then, he would sneak a comment in that left me with lingering doubt. Also I wasn't ready to give up on the Watcher angle just yet.

I drove to Linville on the off chance they would have something in their library that Evergreen did not. Luckily, they had a section on mythology. I found a book entitled *Gods, Goddesses, and Biblical Beings*, took it to a table in the back, and began thumbing through the pages. Most of it focused on Greek and Roman traditions, but there was a small section near the back for all things biblical. I scanned the pages furiously and found a section on Watchers:

Watcher—a term referring to an angelic being who sinned against God and was expelled from the ranks of heaven. They were forced to dwell among mankind as punishment for their transgressions and took for themselves the daughters of men and did populate the earth with extraordinary creatures, half-man, half-angel, the creatures of old. *

Seeing the asterisk, I looked to the bottom of the page for the footnote.

Woe unto you who seek the wisdom of a Watcher, for it is fool's gold and brings with it only folly and despair.

I circled the footnote, tore the page from the book, folded it, then stuffed it into my pocket, assuming no one would miss it.

That night, a colossal thunderstorm hovered over the valley for hours. Lightning danced on the horizon, and thunder echoed in the distance as if the angels were marching into battle. The sweet smell of springtime rains soothed me, so I stayed on the porch until after midnight as I pondered my next move. As usual, my thoughts drifted to Amanda. The idea of her being so far away made me sad, but at least I got to see her a couple of times a week.

Just as I was ready to call it a night, a thought bubbled to the surface. The night Lenny and I were rummaging around in the Rattners' trailer, we took with us two items. First was the shotgun, but the other was the box of seemingly unimportant things. For whatever reason, Lenny had hung on to it and didn't show any of us what was inside. I remembered seeing a couple of IDs, which I presumed were the Rattners' old licenses or library cards, but now that I thought of it, I was curious. But it would have to wait for another time because a wave of exhaustion washed over me.

CHAPTER
SEVENTEEN

THE REVELATION

The spirit is willing but the flesh—well, you know the rest. Finch's trial was a sham and lasted only three days. As expected, the jury convicted him in a matter of hours, and the only thing left now was the sentencing. The judge put a rush on it, claiming it was a special circumstance for the heinous nature of the crime. I knew the truth; it was Mr. Davis who had orchestrated the whole thing. Judge White was set to retire later in the year, and Robert Davis had his eye on his seat. They were thick as thieves, the two of them, and it all but erased whatever faith I had in humanity and the justice system.

School let out for the summer on a Thursday. While my friends relished officially being seniors, my mind was two hundred miles away. It was a three-and-a-half-hour drive from Evergreen to the Duke Hospital in Durham, but I made it in three. Having a temper and a lead foot meant my car was fast when I needed to be, and today it needed to fly.

Amanda was moved from the hospital in Raleigh to the cancer treatment center in Durham so the doctors could monitor her more closely. Cindy spent every day at the hospital, and so did Ronnie when he wasn't working. Their house across the street, which had been so full of life, now sat empty, dark, devoid of life. Even the yellow paint, which had at one time seemed so bright to me, had faded a little. I wondered if things would ever return to normal, but deep down, I knew the answer.

I stopped at the nurse's station and asked for Amanda's room number. A lovely young lady named Evelyn, a redhead who didn't look much older than me, showed me to the end of the hall. I held in my hand a vase of pink carnations—her favorite—and the biggest teddy bear I could find. It was the only thing I had left to offer, other than my company, and that wasn't worth much. My stomach was full of butterflies again, which was always the case when I was around Amanda, but this time it was different.

I steadied myself, cleared my throat, then knocked. "Hey beautiful," I said as I poked my head into the room.

She was lying on her back, staring up at the ceiling. I wondered if she was envisioning the dots in the ceiling like stars. That seemed like something she would do. She turned her head enough to recognize it was me and feebly waved me in. I now noticed a network of tubes and wires connecting her body to machines that beeped and hummed behind the bed. The sight of it shattered what was left of my already broken heart, but I promised myself I would be strong.

"Hey yourself," she said in a raspy voice as she labored a smile. "Is all that for me?"

"It's not too much, is it?"

I helped her sit up in bed and got close enough to press her nose to the flowers. She drew in a long breath and closed her eyes. A hint of a smile worked into the corners of her mouth, and then she fell back onto the pillow.

"No. I love it. Thank you."

"You're welcome." I set the flowers in the sunlight and handed her the bear, which she placed in the bed beside her. Then I grabbed a stool and sat down. "How are you feeling today?"

"Tired," she murmured, "but I'm still here."

Her face was paler than the last time I saw her, and she was swollen, but I didn't care. As long as there was life in her eyes, I knew there was still hope.

"I didn't see your mom or Ronnie—are they here?"

"They left a half hour ago. I think they went to get something to eat." She caught her breath. She got tired quickly these days. "You don't have to keep coming all the way out here just to see me, you know? I know how long a drive it is."

"But I want to."

"You really are sweet, Cole Mercer. I'm sure everyone says so."

I smiled. "Maybe, but it's still nice to hear *you* say it."

There was a long pause, during which I noticed the other flowers, cards, and balloons she had received. They were sitting in the window behind me.

"Someone's popular." I looked at a card from Mr. Hillard, our art teacher.

"There's so many," she said. "Mom and Ronnie had to take most of them home because my room was getting too crowded. I feel bad for everyone spending so much money on me."

"Don't feel bad. Once you get better, you can write them all thank-you letters. How does that sound?"

"Like a dream," she said, smiling again. She paused as her smile melted away. I instantly recognized a change in her mood. She reached for my hand. "I want you to promise me something, Cole." She looked me in the eye.

"Anything." Her hand was frail and icy.

"When this is all over, promise you won't forget me."

She said things like that all the time now, but it didn't make them any easier to hear.

"Don't talk like that," I said, unwilling to let go of the last shred of hope I still clung to like a life raft.

"Cole." She squeezed my hand.

The sound of her voice drew my gaze to hers.

"It's okay." She smiled. "Our time is short, but our memory is long. Please promise me."

I fought back the tears with all the strength I had left in me. I had to be strong now for both of us.

"I promise." I swallowed the lump in my throat. "But you have to promise me something."

"Sure. Anything."

"Promise me you won't give up. I haven't given up on you, and I don't want you to. I know there's still a way."

She smiled sweetly. I knew she didn't believe me, but she agreed anyway.

The nurse came in to check her vitals and give her another round of medicine. She groaned.

"I'm sorry, Cole, but you may have to leave soon," she said begrudgingly. "The medicine makes me feel nauseated, and I don't want you to be here if I get sick to my stomach."

I wanted to stay no matter what happened, but I knew she

wouldn't let me. I supposed she wanted to maintain some shred of dignity.

"How's Kimberly?" she asked as she sat up and swallowed the pills.

"I haven't talked with her since, well, since we broke up."

"She's not still mad, is she?"

"No. I think she's hurt more than anything else, but she's strong. She'll get over it in time. Has she not been to see you yet?"

"Tomorrow."

"Good. I'd hate for the two of you to be at odds." I wanted to add *at the end,* but I still couldn't force my mind to go there.

"You're starting to sound like me," she said.

The shimmer from her eyes was all but gone now, probably permanently, leaving a steely gray that looked cold and uninhabitable. The last of her hair was gone too, but she wore a cap to hide it. I didn't care. I still thought she was the most beautiful creature God had ever let loose on the earth.

"Jackson and Gabe wanted me to tell you hello and Charlie and the entire baseball team," I said with a chuckle. "Everyone is praying for you. I talked to Reverend Ridgeway, and he said he'd hold another meeting of the prayer warriors on Saturday. Every prayer counts." It was at that moment I thought about my dad. Would one more prayer have saved him? There was a time when I thought that was foolish, but now, well, things were different now, and I couldn't be sure anymore.

"That's nice," she said. "Tell them all thank you."

"Oh, we're thinking of making church a regular thing," I announced. "We sat behind your mom and Ronnie on Sunday. Did they tell you?"

"Yes. They mentioned it the other day. That makes me happy." A tear formed in the corner of her eye.

I wasn't sure I liked it any more than the first time I'd gone with her all those months ago, but I had decided I needed it. Despite what I thought about its mechanics, somehow, I at least felt like there was hope when I was there. Without it, I wasn't sure I could go on. "I have you to think for that."

She smiled but said nothing. We sat in silence for a while, unsure of what to talk about. We'd said so many things already, but so many more things were left to be said.

"Did I ever tell you I had the biggest crush on you when you moved here?" She broke the silence.

"You did?"

"Oh yeah," she said. "Remember that first weekend, when I took you to the overlook?"

It had only been the previous summer, but it felt like two lifetimes ago.

"I remember." How could I forget? It was one of my fondest memories.

"I never told you, but I thought you were the most hand-some guy I'd ever laid eyes on. Before you came to town, I never really thought about what my type was, but the first time I saw you, I knew you were it. You were so different from anyone I had ever met."

"Must have been the accent." We both laughed. "Did you know I thought the same thing about you?"

"You did? Why didn't you say anything?"

"I wanted to—tried to—but it just never seemed like the right time. Then there was the whole thing with Rusty and Kimberly and, I don't know..." My voice fell off as I considered all the missed opportunities. "Why didn't you say anything?"

"Same as you, I guess." She sighed. "Would you do it differently if you could... knowing what you know now?"

I considered her question for a few long seconds, and it made me sad. "Yes," I said sincerely. "I should have taken you in my arms and kissed you that first day at the overlook and never let you go." No matter how hard I fought, I could not deny the tears. I used the back of my hand to wipe them from my face.

"I wanted you to."

"You did?"

"Yes. I almost kissed you, but I was afraid," she said, looking regretful.

"Of what?"

She stared off toward the window and thought for a moment, then turned back to me.

"Of falling in love," she answered.

"I don't think we should fear love." I had given the subject a great deal of thought. "There are so many things in life to fear, but God didn't intend for love to be one of them. It should be fearless, unwavering, able to withstand all the pain and suffering life brings."

She gave me a funny look. "You finally hear them, don't you?" she asked as she smiled.

Our eyes met.

"What?"

"The whispers. Can you hear them speaking?" She closed her eyes, the way she had in the woods that day.

It sounded strange, but I knew exactly what she was talking about. Maybe the trees had been speaking to me all along, but I had been unable or unwilling to listen.

Tears streaked down her face.

226

"Please don't cry," I said, wiping them away. "You're so much more beautiful when you're smiling."

Fresh tears fell from both our eyes, and I leaned in and gave her a kiss. The spark, the same one I'd felt the first time I saw her, was still there and strong as ever, and I knew there was still a chance.

"I was wrong about you," she said, composing herself.

I looked at her curiously.

"When I said you had conflict inside you. I don't see that anymore."

I wasn't sure what she saw, but I was as torn as I had ever been. I stayed with her until the medicine kicked in, then she asked if I would go. I told her I needed to be heading back anyway as it would be well after dark before I made it back to Evergreen but promised to return the next day. She said she looked forward to seeing me. Then I told her I loved her, kissed her goodbye, and headed out into the night.

I cried like a baby most of the way home. The idea of what it meant to be strong still eluded me. I had my dad's version of strength, and then I had what I thought was something closer to reality. Real men *did* cry; I'd heard my mom say it many times. It took strength to cry, be vulnerable, and be exposed, and I was only learning how to do this.

It was nearly midnight when I pulled in the drive, but Mom was still up, waiting for me in the kitchen. She could tell I had been crying.

"How was she?" she asked gently. The sound of her voice startled me.

"What are you still doing up?" I asked, shrugging the jacket off my shoulders and sliding it on a hanger in the closet.

"Waiting for you," she whispered. "I needed to know you

were okay." She studied my face carefully. I thought about lying, but she would see straight through it. No one knew me like my mom. After all, every mother's superpower is her intuition. "How is Amanda?"

"Not good." I fought back the tears again, which seemed to have no end. "To be honest, I'm not sure how much longer she has."

"Oh, Cole, I'm so very sorry," she said, rising from the table. She met me in the living room and held me in her arms for a long time, which despite being seventeen, was precisely what I needed. Sometimes I felt alone in this world, like being lost in a dark forest with no way out. I hadn't shown any emotion when my father died, kept it bottled up so no one would think I was weak, but this—this had broken me.

"I've been praying for her," Mom said, holding me a few inches from her. Usually, I would have snapped at her for a comment like that, but I knew Amanda needed all the help she could get, so I thanked her instead.

"I've got to get some sleep." I was suddenly exhausted as the adrenaline subsided. "I'm going back tomorrow."

She tightened her eyes, looking concerned. "I want to make sure you are taking care of yourself."

"I'll be fine."

"Will you?"

"I have to be," I said, resolute. "I don't have a choice."

She pulled back and stood under the archway that separated the kitchen from the living room, as if considering her words before speaking again. "Last year, when I received the phone call about your father, I remember not wanting to believe it. I had always lived my life like I thought God wanted me to. Foolishly, I assumed I would be given a pass. When your dad died, all that changed, and it was only then I realized how fragile life is. What I'm trying to say is, take nothing for granted and leave nothing unsaid, because you don't know if you'll be able to say it tomorrow."

That night I got on my knees and prayed the way any man should when the love of his life was at death's door. It was the hardest thing I'd ever had to do. The chances were unimaginably minuscule, but I asked God to do whatever it took to save Amanda Davenport. I made every promise I could think of to convince him, though I knew that wasn't how it worked. Still, I laid it all on the line that night, pouring my heart out, confessing every transgression I'd ever made until I had nothing left to say or give.

After everyone was asleep, I spent a long time sitting at the end of my bed, thinking and staring off toward the mountain. Spring had turned the trees green again, just as they had been the day we moved in. I thought I even caught a hint of lavender in the air, and it made me smile. The lights were out at Finch's place, so I pulled the covers up around me and tried to sleep.

I waited for a week and hoped beyond hope that my prayer had worked, but after seeing Amanda in that bed, hooked up to so many machines, I feared it was in vain.

I awoke on Saturday. The sky was a foreboding shade of gray, signaling a storm on the horizon. I dressed in jeans and a T-shirt, ate a bowl of cereal, then got in my car, drove down to the Flats, and knocked on Carl Sanders's door. He stood there with the look of a defeated man, and I knew how he felt. I felt sorry for him for the first time and wondered how Lenny's death hadn't broken him completely.

"Mr. Sanders, I'm sorry to bother you, but..."

"Come in, Cole," he said, showing me inside.

For a moment, I thought I was dreaming because the same house I had so reviled was now spotless. The floors had been refinished, fresh paint applied to the walls, and all the holes in the walls patched. Even the smell was pleasant.

"You've been busy," I said.

"After Lenny died, I almost lost it, but your mama talked me into staying with those classes. I finally told God I was done bein' mean. I just wish I'd a done it before..." His voice trailed off, and I thought I saw a tear in his eye.

I didn't like the sight of grown men crying, so I quickly spoke up.

"The reason I came down here... there's a box Lenny had... the night he was..."

Carl disappeared into the kitchen and came back with the box.

"Do you mind?" I asked.

We set it on the table in the living room and lifted the lid. Inside, hidden beneath some old shotgun shells and a half-used pack of cigarettes, were the IDs of the teenagers from Linville. I had been right all along.

"I need you to do something for me," I said as I returned the lid to the box. "Can you take this to the police station at noon? I'd do it myself, but I have an errand to run for my mother."

Carl agreed.

I left the Flats and went straight to the jail to see Finch. When I arrived, he was sitting in his cell at the edge of the bed, eyes cast toward the bare concrete floor. I could only imagine what must be going through his head. His age seemed to rise and fall like the tide and was different each time I saw him, but today he looked much older, and the wrinkles on his face appeared to have doubled, the lines deeper than ever. I stood a safe distance away, so he could not see me, and watched him in silence for several minutes, contemplating what I would say to him. Somehow, I was sure he sensed my presence.

"What are you doing here, Cole?" he asked.

It's an uneasy feeling to stare into the eyes of a man whose days are numbered.

"I wanted to come and see you before they move you." I stepped forward and put my hands on the cold iron bars. "I'm sorry about what happened. I wish there was something I could do to change things."

He let out a small laugh. "Maybe it's better this way."

"I've been thinking." I walked to the end of the cell and stared down the hall. "What if I said I wanted to make a trade?" I paused and waited for him to answer.

He lifted his head and looked at me through bloodshot eyes. It was apparent he had been crying. "What kind of trade?"

"Your freedom for Amanda's life," I said calmly.

"Cole, I already told ya..."

"I tried it your way. I've prayed until I'm blue in the face, but she's dying. I went to visit her yesterday. Without a miracle, she won't last the weekend." I had come so far with Amanda, and I couldn't let her go, not if there was the chance something could be done.

"Cole, you must listen to me now." His voice was calm. "You don't know what you're asking. Whatever you're thinkin', it won't happen that way. You gotta trust me on this."

231

I tried to ignore his words. "I hear what you're saying, but unfortunately, I'm out of time. I must do this now. There is no other way."

"No. I won't do it!"

"But you don't have a choice, do you?"

Any hope he had left in his eyes vanished, leaving in its place only despair. He dropped his gaze and turned away from me.

"Then say it," he demanded coldly. "Say the words!"

I closed my eyes and let out a sigh. "Bishop to e7... checkmate."

Our game was over.

That afternoon, just as I had instructed, Carl Sanders came forward with the box we took from the Rattners' trailer and turned it over to the police. In it were items linking Troy and Tommy Rattner to the murders of the Linville Three. It's funny. In the end, Lenny got the best of them, just like he said he would. I couldn't help but smile and look at the sky, hoping he was smiling back.

Robert Davis had to eat an awful lot of crow that day and reluctantly ordered Old Man Finch to be released. When they went to tell him the news, that old bird had flown the coop, in a matter of speaking.

That night, I had a dream that terrified me more than any other in my life. I was standing at the foot of a grave in a vast cemetery. As far as I could see, there were headstones, pearl white, rising and falling with the ground in undulating waves. It reminded me of the time my dad had taken me to Arlington National Cemetery. The names etched into the stones were all the people I had met over the years. I searched the tombstones, looking for one name in particular—my own, but it was not among them. I woke in a cold sweat and wondered what it meant.

The next afternoon, I went up to the mountain hoping beyond hope that Mr. Finch would be there, but I knew better. He was gone for good this time. I placed the white bishop back on the board and returned the pieces to their starting positions. The next game would have to wait.

I made it back home just in time to hear the phone ring. It was Cindy Davenport. She said I needed to get to the hospital quick.

Cindy and Ronnie were in the waiting room when I arrived, along with Reverend Ridgeway and half the school. Everyone looked up at me as I entered. I felt a little like a soldier walking into battle against an enemy that had me outnumbered. I feared the worst. "Is she—?" I couldn't bring myself to say it.

"She's been waiting... for you." Cindy forced the words out.

This was the moment I had been dreading since she first told me she was sick. Everything that had happened had led me, us, to this moment. My brain was crystal clear now. I pressed off down the hall to her room. I felt different this evening. My heart was lighter. I stopped at the door and looked over my shoulder—the living behind me, the dead ahead—and I found myself caught somewhere in the middle. The moment was too poignant to be amusing. I drew in a breath and entered the room. She was asleep. I stood in the doorway for a minute and watched her breathing, overly thankful for something as simple as seeing her chest heave and fall with regularity.

I sat quietly in the chair and watched her while she slept.

Her face, still angelic and perfect, was just as it had been that first day in the woods. I didn't have the heart to wake her, so I just sat in her presence and thanked God for the time with her. Late in the evening, when the sun was nearly gone, I saw her eyelids flutter. Her fingers had been entwined with mine for the longest time, and I felt the slightest twitch that let me know she was still with me.

"Amanda," I whispered softly. My voice was shaky. "Amanda, are you awake?"

She stirred at the sound of my voice. Her eyelids fluttered again, but this time she found the strength to open them.

"There you are," I breathed.

"Cole?" she whispered.

"It's me. I'm here." I squeezed her hand.

"I was having the strangest dream," she began. "I was standing in a garden, and I was surrounded by beautiful flowers. Someone was there with me. I couldn't see his face, but his voice was so strong, like the roar of a thousand oceans. He told me not to worry, that everything was going to be okay."

I felt a shiver climb my spine. "Have the nurses been by to check on you?" I asked, noticing only now that the machines were gone.

"They stopped giving me medicine this morning. They said they would try to make me as comfortable as they could."

I knew what that meant. Somewhere in my mind, I searched for words of wisdom, but none came. All I could do now was watch and wait. "Mr. Finch got released from jail this morning. I thought you might like to know that."

"That's wonderful." She stared at me. "You did it. I knew you could."

"I want you to know how much I love you," I said.

Her eyes reddened, and although the tears were difficult to come by these days, a solitary tear grew in the corner of her eye, then streamed in a long streak down the side of her face.

"I love you too," she whispered, barely able to get the words out without getting choked up.

"This isn't fair." I was indignant, thinking of all that was possible between us.

"Life isn't fair," she replied.

"I want you to know I'll be here with you the whole time. I won't leave your side anymore."

She squeezed my hand.

We sat in silence for a long time. As the sun faded, I read passages from Emily Dickinson as she drifted in and out of consciousness. Then, somewhere close to midnight, she floated off to the place where the trees spoke in a language all their own.

That night, in a hospital room in the middle of North Carolina, Amanda Davenport and I, two souls adrift on an endless sea of darkness, found one another and held on for dear life.

CHAPTER
EIGHTEEN

EVERGREEN

At dawn the next morning, I woke to find Amanda sitting up in bed.

"Amanda, you're..."

"Better." And when she smiled at me, my heart was full.

"But how—?"

"Last night I had the strangest dream," she said. "There was a light hovering just above the bed. I think that maybe it was an angel. And from the light came a voice that told me everything was going to be okay. When I woke this morning I felt different, as if the cancer had somehow been taken away." She squeezed my hand. "See, miracles do happen, if only you believe."

THE DOCTORS and nurses had no explanation for it, calling it the miracle of all miracles. There was even a big write-up about it in the *Raleigh Times*, which I had framed and keep to this very day. Over the years, everyone I told that story to said that she must have had faith like Job, but I like to think cancer simply wasn't willing to take a creature as extraordinary as Amanda Davenport.

A week after her brush with death, we walked out of that hospital in Durham, hand in hand, and never looked back. We dated the rest of the summer and the year after, and when high school was over, I asked Amanda Gertrude Davenport to marry me on the overlook above the town. Once upon a time, she said it was her favorite place in the world, and I supposed it was mine too. So much of our story had been told there.

We talked about moving away from Evergreen once or twice, but when our son Alex was born in '92 and Emma came along three years later, we decided we might as well stay. We wanted our kids to have a life like we had, filled with family, friends, and enduring love. For sixty-three years, we never left one another's side, until the day she slipped away from me for the last time.

I buried Amanda in the White Hall cemetery beside her mother, Ronnie, and my sister Tabitha, who died in a car accident with her best friend Darlene when they were seventeen. Many of the friends I once knew are buried there, too.

Heartbroken, my mother moved away from Evergreen not long after Tabitha died and met a godly man named Mike Houser, a physician from Atlanta, who helped her through the grieving. They were married a year later and spent the next forty years living life to the fullest and taking nothing for granted. I was at her side when she took her last breath at the ripe old age of ninety-three.

Jackson and Gabe left Evergreen after high school. They

regularly visited for a while, then life got in the way, and eventually, they stopped coming altogether. Gabe died of a heart attack at forty-two, leaving behind his wife Janette and their two little girls. Jackson and I were pallbearers at his funeral. It was one of the saddest things I've ever had to do. I saw Jackson years later when his mom passed. His hair had turned gray, and he was going through a divorce. We reminisced about that summer I moved to Evergreen and remembered fondly the flood, the festival, the time we faced our fear and stood up to the Rattners, and the night poor Lenny paid the ultimate price for it.

Charlie Hammond worked for a media conglomerate in Chicago and was, for a time, one of the wealthiest men in the state of Illinois. I saw him only once after high school, but he was fat and happy.

The Shoffner twins went on to both play baseball for the Greenville Braves. I was in attendance the night Eric made it to the big leagues. He pitched a shutout.

THIS MORNING, a thick fog hangs on Spar Mountain. By noon, the sun will win out like it always does, but until then, I relish the time spent in the mist. The mountain is my world now, and I tend to it like any good shepherd would, with patience and understanding. I work the land, repair the house when it needs fixing, and in the evenings, when I feel up to it, I sit down to supper and a game of chess. But it can be awfully lonely up here in the clouds. It's been twenty years since I've talked to another living soul, and sometimes the silence is so loud I talk to myself just to keep from going mad.

At night, I leave the light on in memory of Thaddeus Finch, the greatest man I ever knew. I think about the first time I met him and how frightened I was of that shotgun, how scared I was the night I took it to save Lenny's life, and how it paled in comparison to the fear I felt when I stole it back. Then I think about the trade we made there in that jail, a life for a life, and how that changed everything.

These days, I long for spring and the hope that someone will find the courage to climb the mountain. If I'm lucky, they'll want to play a game of chess with a tired old man. Until that day comes, I'll be right here praying, not for a bountiful life the way I did when I was a young man, but for death. I suppose if I think on it long enough, perhaps I am dead, and this is my hell. After all, it's a razor's edge we walk between life and death, good and evil, heaven and hell. I'm just glad my dear Amanda isn't here to see it.

As I look out into the fog, I think about all the friends and family I've watched die over the years. It's a strange feeling to know you're the last of the ones you know, and even stranger to realize your turn will never come. I'll be a hundred-seventy-one next year, ten years older than Finch was when I took his place. As I think back on that chess match we had all those years ago, I wonder if he didn't win after all.

Then I think back on that night when I laid bare my soul before God and asked him to heal Amanda, and how I also asked him to save me from the darkness she had seen that day in the woods. It's funny how some prayers get answered and others don't. Perhaps God has a sense of humor after all. There's no way to know how Amanda was saved. Sometimes I think I had a hand in it, or Finch, or both, and other times I think it might have been all those people who prayed for her.

Maybe it was God himself who touched her and made her whole, but only he knows the answer.

It's been almost a century since I last held the hand of the only girl I ever loved—that beautiful, delicate creature for whom there never was and never will again be a match on this earth or in the heavens above, and while time dulls the memory, it only sharpens the sting of the loss.

Not much is left of Evergreen, I'm afraid, except a few abandoned buildings and one or two houses on the Bluff that continue to fight a losing battle against nature and time. A few years after Amanda passed, another flood, worse than the one in '86, washed half the town away. Those who survived packed up and moved to Linville or Burnsville and left Evergreen to wither on the vine. The church is gone too, destroyed in a storm I swore was the beginning of the end, but the cemetery survived and stands as a reminder of a time long since passed.

Now and then, when I feel up to it, I come down from the mountain and lay a flower on the graves of all those souls I once knew. I walk the streets and close my eyes and try my best to remember, but it's been so long. On my way back up, I always stop at the overlook and run my fingers across the initials we carved into that hemlock tree, which still stands today. Then it all comes flooding back; that love that is and forever will be evergreen. As for me, I'm resigned to my fate, at eternity on the mountain, waiting, watching, and praying for someone to relieve me of my duty.

END

PLEASE LEAVE A REVIEW/SHARE ON SOCIAL MEDIA

Thank you for reading *Evergreen*. If you have an opportunity, please leave an honest review on your preferred platform. For those on TikTok, feel free to share on #BookTok. In the meantime, please check out Buck's other stories at:

www.buckturner.com

Made in United States
Cleveland, OH
12 November 2024

10604056R20146